MW01242007

BID NOT, FOR MY LOVE

Darcee Tana

All rights reserved

DEDICATE

To the reader

My grateful thanks –

To my family, for enduring a writer

To my parents, for inspiring a writer

To my in-laws, for accepting a writer

To my friends, for encouraging a writer

This is a work of fiction. Names, characters, places and incidents are the product of the author's imagination. Any resemblance to actual persons, living or dead, business establishments, events or locales is entirely coincidental.

Except for use in reviews, no part of this work may be reproduced or utilized by any electronic, mechanical or other means, including xerography, photocopying and recording, or used in any information storage or retrieval system, without the permission of the author

Cover photos courtesy of Darja Vorontsova & Valery Sibrikov; dreamstime.com
Cover by Jolene Naylor

Copyright @2011 Darcee Tana

Chapter 1

"RAUL! Ye will do as I say son. Ye will marry, for ye are a man of thirty now. The past is over and it cannot be undone. Rosalie is wedded to another. We did what we thought was right, ye cannot hold that against us for eternity or punish me by choosing the path of a Templar Knight."

"Nay father, ye did what yer bride wanted. I have not the wish to marry. I do not now. I will not in the future." Raul calmly responded, though his hour long conversation with his father had tested his patience to its limit.

"And who will carry my name after ye? Everything I have striven to maintain will pass to my cousin's son. Is that what ye desire?" his father, Lord Bruce of Wilbert's voice was laced with pain.

"Father, I had planned to wed Rosalie. Together we would have given ye the heir ye desire. Instead of granting my wish, ye chose to separate us. And now ye plan an alliance with yer bride's niece, with full knowledge that ye condemn me to hell. I cannot let ye sacrifice my life, a second time." Raul spoke with determination in his voice.

"I was thinking of yer future, son. Rosalie was our mason's daughter. Is that the tie ye wished to forge? She had fooled ye with all that nonsense about love. Ye were a mere youth Raul. Ye were but eighteen. Every man of that age, believes he has found the great love of his life, only to know years later, it was but a youthful folly. I could not let ye make that mistake. Much depended on ye, son, much depended on ye" His father said trying to justify his actions.

"And ye do not think, that yer marriage to Ma'am is equally deserving of the term, folly?" Raul retaliated.

"Raul! I was much older than ye. And much wiser! Ye needed a mother, and she wanted to be a mother to ye" Lord Wilbert repeated the argument he had made several times in as many years.

"I had, a mother. Ye compelled me to accept another in that role. That father was yer first folly. Now ye want me to accept her niece in the role of my bride. That father will be yer second." Raul knew that he should have simply left, instead of expressing his view, but now that the subject had been raised, he had to say his piece.

"Folly! Ye dare talk about folly. The only folly I committed was is in letting ye mix with 'that' woman, Rosalie. Were it not for Maja, our family would have been shackled with her. Ye owe Maja yer gratitude for getting Rosalie wedded in time ...."

Raul saw red at the knowledge that the woman responsible for his mother's heartache was now equally responsible for his.

"With what authority father, did ma'am do that?" he shouted back.

"With the authority, that belongs to my bride! I gave her the authority to look to the safe keeping of our family's name."

Raul burst out laughing. 'Father, our family's name was no longer an issue after ye wed the woman..."

"That is enough Raul. I have long ceased the attempt to bring about any civil relations between Maja and ye. My only desire now is that ye take yer responsibility seriously. Remember that both, the title and my land will come to ye when I am gone. But ye must prove yerself worthy. Son, I declare now that if ye do not marry, ye will forfeit the title and land that should rightfully be yers. I will leave all to Maja's nephew. Of late he is more of a son to me than ye." Raul was determined to force his son into accepting the alliance and this threat was the thing he hoped would bring his son to his senses.

"If that be so father, then it is best I take yer leave and establish my home in Kinsborough." Raul spoke quietly yet firmly. With what he planned for his future he did not need Wilbert. It would be more of a burden for him, than an asset.

"Kinsborough? Yer home is here!" his father ejected, realising that his ploy had not worked at all and he stood to lose, more than before.

"Nay father, my home is where my wishes are respected and honoured. That home is in Kinsborough. My mother's home, left to me, by her father. We each father, must find our kin, in whom we meet, for nature does not always provide one for us. Like ye, I too found another to fill yer role. My grandfather was more of a father to me. I bid ye goodbye, My Lord. Today ye not only lost mo a father, ye lost yerself a son." With that, Raul bowed and exited the room.

His departure left Lord Bruce in turmoil. He had not wished this outcome. He desired to see his son wed and ready to take on the responsibilities that would soon be his. He had been unwell of late, tiring easily, weakening of strength. All he had wanted was to force his son, into forming an alliance. Maja's niece was not the only alliance that had come. Two neighbouring lords had suitable daughters. A wealthy baron was keen to have Raul wed his child. Lord Bruce could not comprehend, how Raul could throw away his future, over a mere woman. He never believed that Raul truly loved Rosalie. He still felt it was Raul's way of annoying Maja.

His son had never liked Maja, which was understandable since he had married Maja soon after his first bride, Christina's death. He had loved Christina well enough but it was Maja who made him feel alive. Christina was the quiet beauty that graced his home; Maja was the vivacious temptress that enlivened his life. He had not hidden his relationship with Maja from Christina, and she had never expressed any objection to his liaison. Christina had seemed happy, caring for her son and looking after Wilbert.

Raul had always been close to his mother and at her passing, felt her loss deeply. His dislike for Maja had increased with each passing day as he saw Maja take on more and more of Christina's role. Maybe he should have waited longer and ensured Raul was confident of his love for his son. It was too late to go back to that moment now.

To avoid the strain his son was placing on his marriage, as soon as Raul turned thirteen, he had placed him in the care of his friend Maximillian the Brave. A man who had naught, yet had risen to knighthood, with his strength and valour! Raul had lived in Maximillian's castle and trained to become a knight. Bruce loved Maximillian as a brother, and trusted the care of his most precious son to him. That truth did little to improve his relationship with his son.

Raul grew into a strong lad, clever of wit, endowed with strength and remained handsome of features. At eighteen he returned home. And that was when the problem began. Raul fell in love with their mason's daughter, Rosalie. Seeing it as a mere dalliance, Lord Bruce had not intervened. When Maja and he realised that the two were planning to wed, he ensured that Rosalie was wedded off by her father to a respectable knight some shires away. He learnt too late that the knight was much older than Rosalie or he would have found her another. He had wanted her out of his son's life but he had not wished her sacrificed.

Hell had broken loose when Raul, learnt of her marriage. Heartbroken he went and joined the king's battles. Captured by the enemy, he spent a year in captivity, brutally tortured and physically disfigured. In their second year of captivity, three knights escaped - Raul, and two other knights who had formed an unbreakable tie, bonded by their mutual suffering and companionship. The men that returned with him, came bearing the names of Sir Peter and Sir Rowan. The three spent a year in the home of a Hospitaller healing from their injuries. Two more battles followed. More injuries were incurred and more healing was required. During that entire period of nearly a decade, Raul not once contacted his father.

When finally Raul returned to Wilbert, he had no resemblance to the youth that had left a decade before. Still powerful of body and disciplined of mind, he brought with him confidence and the mark of a leader. Raul had become a man.

The only part of this near perfect son, that worried Raul, was his desire to apply for membership to the Order of the Knights Templar. The vow of chastity was not what he wanted for his son. He needed his son to give him the future heir of Wilbert. The child who would carry on his line and name.

As blessings come, Raul was called away by his maternal grandfather, who being near to death and without a male child of his own, wished to declare Raul as his successor. Another year passed and Raul's decision to apply was further delayed.

After a year of ill health, the Baron of Kinsborough died, leaving the responsibility of Kinsborough and its people to Raul. He also passed on the title of Baron to his grandson.

Raul had spent a lot of time at his grandfather's castle while the old Baron ailed. He was joined by his two friends, Sir Peter and Sir Rowan. At his grandfather's death, Raul gave each a portion of his land and the manor built on it. Sir Peter became Sir Peter of Kinsley and Sir Rowan belonged to Kinsmay, Each manor lay just an hour away from Kinsborough Castle and even when they were not fighting at battle, they spent a lot of time together. They offered the King of England their allegiance and their sword arm. As brothers they stood, as friends, they defended.

Lord Bruce's own relationship with Raul was always cordial but devoid of any true warmth from his son. Raul's relationship with Maja was always civil but laced with distrust. Worse still, even after becoming a baron, Raul continued his dream of becoming a Templar Knight.

What was needed was a bride for Raul who would make him forget that dream. Maja had suggested her brother's daughter, but Raul continued to avoid matrimony.

Another year had passed in this stalemate and then this morning's argument had occurred. Lord Bruce well knew that as Raul's father, he should not have given the ultimatum. At this stage in his life, it was he who needed his son. The days when his son needed him were long gone. But the fear of seeing his son join the Order had prompted him to act. And now with his ultimatum, he had gambled on a very risky hand. He would either have an heir to succeed his son or he would not even have that son at all.

## Chapter 2

Raul left his father's home, seething with anger. Truly Maja had played her cards well. If he married her niece, Maja would reign supreme, and if his father declared Maja's nephew as his successor, Maja would remain in control. Either way, she had secured her position.

He had no wish to marry. He had once, many years ago, to Rosalie. It was the first time he had thought of marriage and the more it upset Maja, the more determined he had become to wed Rosalie.

Then one summer he returned from Kinsborough, his mother's childhood home, to find the Rosalie had left, wedded to another man, by her father. Heartbroken he too left the place that held the memories. He knew even then that Maja had a hand in it, but could not prove it. Now he had the proof but with it came the knowledge that his father was equally to blame.

As he galloped his destrier towards Kinsborough he released the anger he held for so long. Spurring his steed to race faster, he covered ground quicker than ever before. But Kinsborough was almost four hours away and so he stopped at St. Ives to give his beloved destrier, Daktonian a rest. He too wished to stretch his legs.

A local farmer offered mead, bread and cheese for him and hay for his destrier. This Raul gladly accepted and gave the farmer coin in exchange. While he ate, he pondered on his situation and searched for the solution.

He was certain that he did not want Wilbert, his father's hold, but it angered him to know that Maja would finally take all that should have been his mothers. And that final insult to his mother was something he would not allow. But to wed? That was not a possibility. To be a Templar Knight, chastity was a vow that had to be fulfilled. And a wedded man could not apply to the Order. Deciding that marriage was too big a sacrifice he declared to himself that on reaching Kinsborough he would formally apply to the Order, just as Peter had already done.

Raul, ran his fingers through his windblown hair, a habit that he found, relaxed him.

While Daktonian quenched his thirst, Raul's attention was drawn to the scene by his left, where three women were being dragged along the central road. Their hands tied by a thick twine, they were prodded by the man following them, with his sword, as inducement to speed up their gait.

Raul rose. As a knight sworn to defend a woman's honour he made his way slowly toward the crowd that was gathering. If they had committed theft, he would be unable to protect them from their punishment but if they were innocent women, he knew that he would have to secure their freedom.

Daktonian neighed loudly, and Raul turned towards his destrier. Daktonian had his hind leg caught in a vine. The more he wrestled to be free, the tighter the vine, bound his leg. His beloved steed became his first priority. So Raul attended to him first, carefully cutting away the vine and releasing his hind leg. As soon as his destrier was free, he moved to safer ground. All the while, he worked at rescuing Daktonian; Raul could hear cheering from the crowd. Women bound by their hands, was erroneous; the cheering while they were in that state was ominous. He slowly walked back towards the noise.

As he reached the crowd, he noticed that two of the women were being led away by a couple of men. The men leering at the women, spoke in vulgar terms and made crude actions. At the center of the crowd, a third woman stood, her hand wrapped around her waist, gripping tightly to her sides. Her tie had been removed, though the rope around her waist remained. Her face was smudged with dirt. Her hair, clinging to her scalp was a greasy mess and her dusty clothes were torn in several places. But it was her terrified eyes that arrested his attention. It was the same look that he had seen in the eyes of the captives as the enemy came to take them to the torture cells.

The woman looked around at the crowd, as if studying the mood of the people and seeking the escape routes. She lowered them as a man raised his hand and then another followed him. All the signs of a sale were visible, and Raul realised that the bidding was already in progress. Selling a woman was no longer permitted yet the practice continued when law was not represented. He whistled softly and saw Daktonian race to his side. Swiftly he climbed into his saddle.

"I believe this sale is not lawful." Raul called out.

The bidders gave him an angry look before one replied "if ye cannot afford the wench, it is best ye do not meddle." A woman standing beside the first bidder shouted, "I need a maid and she looks healthy and strong enough for work." A man sniggered at her choice of words. Then one by one, the men in the circle displayed their swords as a silent warning for him to take note.

Raul could have fought them but even an able knight like himself, knew his limitations. To take on fifteen men would not be easy, especially when the woman stood bound and at the mercy of her seller.

So Raul was forced to stand silently while the bids continued. When it finally stagnated and he sensed that the men were unable to bid much higher, he put in his bid. Double, what had been offered before! A hush fell over the crowd. The swords went out of view. The seller blinked twice at his bid, surprise written all over his face. And the woman! She lifted her head in one quick motion and looked directly at him. A moment later she had lowered her eyes to her hands again. But in that one moment, Raul realised, that even at a time when she was helpless and an object of sale, her eyes clearly said, for her, there would be no acceptance.

Unwilling to lose the sale price, her seller quickly closed the deal. Just at the moment when Raul handed the seller the coins, with the swiftness of a gazelle, the woman bolted away towards a paddock. While the twine around her waist and her torn garment offered impediments to her attempt, it did not stop that attempt or her speed.

What did stop her, was the seller who chased after her, and on reaching her clobbered her on the side of her head, sending her reeling to the ground. "Ye will pay for yer disobedience wench" he yelled while the crowd cheered once again. He removed the rope attached to his waist. The crowd voiced their encouragement by cheering even louder. Terror invaded the woman's eyes; a terror that told Raul that she had been beaten before.

"Touch her and ye forfeit yer life." Anticipating another barbaric act, Raul had moved closer to the pair and was now facing them when he bellowed those words.

"But Sir, she deserves to be punished." the man replied

"That decision is now mine to take. Ye have completed the sale and she, belongs to me." Raul voiced loudly so that the crowd was also made aware that he had staked his claim.

"Believe me Sir; I have seen many like her, only the whip makes them obey." the seller continued.

"Release her" Raul barked. When that was not done, he barked louder "NOW!"

"Ye are making a mistake Sir. As soon as I let go of the woman, she will run." the seller continued.

"If she runs, ye can have her back" Raul replied, his eyes now meeting that of the woman. He ensured that the woman understood exactly what he was saying and what the repercussions would be, if she bolted again.

"But Sir, ye have already paid for her, ye cannot have yer money back." the seller had no wish to lose out on a handsome deal and let go of her, as if that act made her non-returnable.

"As a gentleman I would not dishonor our deal, however dishonourable the deal itself was. If she bolts again, ye can have her and the money." Raul continued to look at the woman, challenging her to repeat her move. She didn't, even when her ropes were cut, she stood, as still as a statue.

"Ye may leave us now." Raul turned to the seller. The man rushed back to the crowd who continued to stand and watch the spectacle.

"I am going to ride towards the valley. Ye are going to follow me until we are out of their sight. If ye run, I will not follow ye. They will! Do ye understand what I say?" Raul spoke in a hushed tone.

The woman nodded, but did not utter a word. Her nod was enough. Gently he urged Daktonian forward. He did not look back, but the footsteps assured him of her progress.

Heaving a sigh of relief, Raul continued until he could no longer hear the crowd. A quick glance assured him that they were out of sight too. He stopped as soon as he had a second glance.

As he turned to look at the woman, she gently whistled, and an old palfrey, moved slowly towards her.

Raul frowned. A bonded woman, with a palfrey! An interesting combination. He decided to query it.

"How is it, that ye have this animal?" Raul questioned.

The woman hesitated, then in a voice no more than a whisper, replied, "She belonged to my father. It is all I have left of him." Her voice was clear. The language used correctly. This brought another frown to his brow.

While the palfrey was not a magnificent creature like Daktonian, it would still be a valuable property. He knew she spoke no truth and hoped that she had not stolen the animal. For the moment however, it was going to solve the problem of their mode of travel. The woman was not slim and he was wondering how she would manage riding on his destrier with him. She also had an obnoxious odour that followed her and he had dreaded being seated in close proximity.

Sensing that she was going to be allowed to ride her palfrey, she led it towards some boulders.

He watched as she then stood on the larger one and climbed onto the mare's back. Seated safely, she guided her animal behind his, glancing every few minutes to see if the crowd had reappeared.

She was right to be wary, for a small band of men were now once again visible, though still maintaining a distance.

"Follow me until I say so. Do not speak to me. Do not look at me. And keep yer head down." Raul commanded without looking back. Another in her situation would have done that automatically but he had seen defiance in her eyes in those few moments after his bid. It was likely that she would respond differently and force him into a battle with the men that now followed them.

Luckily for him, without uttering a single word, the woman obeyed his every command.

Only when they reached the next village, an hour away and noting that the crowd no longer followed, Raul stopped. He alighted by a small stream and let Daktonian have a drink while he pondered on his next action.

The woman remained seated on her palfrey.

"Yer palfrey needs a drink as well. Let her do so now for there is no other source for many miles." He informed her.

The woman, still remaining seated, guided her palfrey to the stream so that it too, could drink with Daktonian.

"Where were ye planning to go?" Raul asked, while he looked on.

"Sir, I need to get to The Abbey of St. Mary" she whispered. When Raul did not reply, she repeated it again, louder this time and in a commanding tone.

"How is it that ye speak our language so well? And why is it that ye command, when not a short while ago ye stood, offered for sale?" he retorted. He had already had a belly full of orders from one woman. He did not want that from another.

"I do not command Sir, I but request." she replied with feigned meekness.

"Ye would be best to remember, that a request must be uttered with humility. Ye add authority and ye will make it sound, an order." he pronounced

"Aye sir" she whispered.

"And, yer language?" he asked. She thought he had forgotten. He has the satisfaction of noting her dismay at having the same question addressed again.

"My father was a steward. I learnt with the lady of the house." another lie passed through her lips

"Steward ye say, to whom? Raul asked.

"To Lord Agnus of Melsville, sir." Lord Agnus did not personally know her. But she knew of him and his was the first name that had come to her mind. Melsville was a small village in the south of the country of no real importance other than Lord Agnus being recently wed to her distant cousin. A cousin she had not met. The knight asked too many questions, and she had to be careful to keep her identity a secret until she reached the Abbey.

"Melsville? I have not heard of it" Raul suspected a lie, for she referred to Angus as Lord, yet Melsville, his holding seemed insignificant, for he was not aware of it.

"Not many people have Sir. It is near our southern shores." she explained.

"How is it then that ye came to be with 'that' man? Where is yer father?" Raul queried further. As a steward's daughter she may not command the same protection as a lady, however women did not travel alone, no matter what their standing in society.

"My father died some moons ago Sir. I was being sent to the north but our party was attacked soon after we left. I was captured by the man who sold me to ye." She replied evenly, but Raul could see the slight tremor that accompanied her words.

"What of the other two women? Were they from yer party? Raul continued his line of questioning.

"Nay sir, they were captives before our party was attacked." she answered

"How many men attacked yer party." Raul needed to know this information so that he could plan his attack should they appear again.

"Five men, Sir, Two of the men were standing amidst the crowd. The man who addressed ye, was one of them." she furnished.

Raul instinctively knew, that she was passing on vital information and that it was being done with intent. Like him, she expected the party to attack again and was warning him of the odds.

Five men in the vicinity and all of them armed and as far as he knew, three were still together. He would have to save his queries for a later moment. If they were to be safe they would have to hurry, for safety lay within the walls of Kinsborough.

Battling five men would be an easy feat for a knight of his capability but when there was a woman to defend as well, the task almost becomes insurmountable. Many a knight has died defending women not because he was not able, but because the damsel in distress was effectively used as bait.

"Where do ye go now?" Raul asked for her destination again, wondering if she had lied before.

"I was told to go to The Abbey of St Mary." She remarked, taking note of his game.

"For what purpose?" he queried

"It was my father's last command Sir" Her father had been adamant that if anything happened to him, she must make her way to the Abbey. The Abbey was a safe haven for women like herself who were without a protector. It isolated them from the men who could harm them. And without her father and brother, harm surrounded her from all quarters. Her aunt once removed, also resided there.

"The Abbey is many days ride from here. I am happy to ride with ye as far as Kinsborough." he offered.

"Thank ye Sir, for yer kindness." Even as she expressed her gratitude, she wondered why he had bought her if he meant to let her go. She must have visibly expressed her query when she frowned, for he answered that query himself.

"Ye are wondering why I bought ye. It was the only way to take ye from them without a battle. I neither need a mistress nor a maid." He spoke with frankness. Had she not wanted to be free, she would have taken it for an insult.

"Sir, on reaching the Abbey, I will repay ye for my price." the woman said, then quickly looked away.

"Ye have that much coin?" he asked, again confounded that a bonded woman spoke of personal wealth.

"Not now Sir, but I soon will." was her response.

"Do not worry about it." He waved off her offer.

"I was put up for sale against my wish sir. Ye bought me against yers. As long as the auction price remains unpaid, I will consider myself in yer debt sir. I wish not to be that, to ye sir or to any man." she said

"Do not consider yerself as bought. The other path in front of me was one of bloodshed. I was morally forced to bid, in order to prevent someone else buying ye. It should not worry ye. Maybe one day ye can do likewise" He remarked.

"But Sir, no one would put a man up for sale?" she sounded perplexed.

Raul stared at her. Then anger seemed to take over his countenance "Ye are wrong in that, my father just did." he snapped.

When next he looked at the woman, she had withdrawn with fear. Raul did not feel the need to apologise or explain his outburst to the woman. Instead he remarked.

"If ye need to have some privacy, this is the time to do so. Once we ride again, we must not stop until we reach Kinsborough. The path is not always safe and I would reach before dark. If those men plan to attack again, they must not be far behind."

With that Raul took hold of Daktonian's reign and swung himself onto the stallion's back. Then silently he rode some distance away.

When the woman alighted, he took a moment to observe her. She was quite plump with patchy skin that seemed to be of several shades. Her dark hair was greasy and tied back into a harsh knot. Her clothes were well worn, torn in several places and made of a think brown woolen material. It was ill fitting, as they usually were when such garments were given after they had been well used by the original owners. And then, there was the odour that surrounded her which he was finding very hard to bear. He recognised it now as the smell of animal fat, the kind of smell that accompanied the burning of tallow candles. The awful smell was the very reason, he had forbidden the burning of tallow candles at Kinsborough instead introducing the use of beeswax candles and oil burners.

Bringing his attension back to the lady in front of him, he noted further that her features were very plain. Had she been a true lady, those plain features would have had to be supported by a large dowry, in order to see her wed. He could understand why she was being sent to the Abbey. It would have been the cheaper alternative for her father. And as a man he could see why another would prefer to stay unwed, than be wed to one, such as her.

WED! The thought made him sit upright.

Why had he not thought of it before? It was the perfect, solution.

His father wanted him married. Well he would fulfill his father's demand. But he would be married on his term, not his fathers. And he had found the most imperfect woman, now offering him the most perfect solution. He laughed aloud. He could not wait to see his father's face when he presented his bride. A bride, who would bring with her, neither birth, breeding, beauty nor wealth. And more importantly, no heir!

When the woman returned, Raul looked at her with a different view. How mad, this woman, would make Maja and his father. A most unsuitable bride! A most suitable revenge!

This woman would put Maja's well-conceived plan to naught. And Raul could not wait to see it happen.

Aye, she was the perfect weapon, and one who already felt indebted to him. He had saved her from untold horror; it was time for her, to save him from his unfathomable hell.

## Chapter 3

They rode in silence, trotting when the terrain was flat and maneuvering with care when the surface got rocky. Raul chose to avoid travelling on the open roads as that would have made them easy targets. He noted the woman express fear when he suggested they get off the main path, but must have realised the logic of his reasoning for she did not query him further nor delay their journey with her hesitation.

During the entire trip, Raul remained silent, concentrating on the sounds around him. Daktonian's ability to pick up on the smallest of sounds was undeniable, however even Daktonian needed quiet, to be able to hear clearly.

Despite his intention to continue the journey uninterrupted, they did make another quick stop and then tried to make up the lost time by riding harder on the plains. Emma's mare could not keep up with Daktonian and on the woman's urging, Raul had to slow down and keep pace with the mare.

Another two hours into the ride, when the sun had lowered itself in the sky, he finally lessened their pace to a canter. While Kinsborough was still some distance away, he was inside his safe haven. The villages they would pass now were known to him. The terrain was one that he could follow blind folded.

Raul realised that there was one question that neither had asked of the other - their names. He broke his silence with that very query, "What is yer name?"

In response to his query, he was given the name of his intended, of just two syllables "Emma". She did not ask his, and he decided to withhold that information.

Emma had already judged him to be a knight. His destrier spoke of his standing. His garment and armour spoke of his status. A confident knight, who carried his spangenhelm tied to his destrier rather than on his head, but a knight travelling without a squire or men, meant that he was a lesser knight, bound to a Lord. And it was the 'Lords' that she feared most.

Had the fear of the five men not rested in her heart, she would have attempted another escape. But one devil was better than five. And she still had her Rondel dagger tied to her waist which promised her some measure of protection.

Just as the sun began to set, Kinsborough came into view. The grey walls of the fortified fort, stood over fifty feet tall. Built on a hilltop, it still did, what it was meant to do: deter an attack from an enemy, and command awe from a friend.

The barbican supporting the drawbridge was impressively set another ten feet higher. A moat surrounded the castle wall. And on the barbican, stood three figures all armed with cross-bows and looking in their direction.

The sight of the impressive structure filled Raul's heart with pride. This was home now for him. His domain, his inheritance and most of all, it was the link with his mother and grandfather.

Emma on the other hand, found her heart pounding against her ribcage. Apprehension made her pull at Athena's reigns. Her palfrey stopped.

Raul turned towards her and once again saw fear displayed on her countenance. He would even have described that look, again as terror.

"Ye need not fear Emma. No one will hurt ye here. Ye are now under my protection." he tried to reassure her.

At that moment the gate was lifted and the drawbridge lowered. Just as the drawbridge touched the ground across the moat, several riders rode out towards them with two, ahead of the rest.

Emma could not accept his assurance. Too many lords had let her down already. Despite his pledge, she knew he would not be able to protect her against his lord. A mere knight did not have that power. Once the men reached her, there would be no escape. She had to make her move now.

Before the next blink of her eye, she had turned her palfrey and begun to gallop away, not knowing where she was going or how her palfrey would ever outride their destriers. Blindly she raced, and then quickly glanced back once, to see Raul stare unbelievingly in her direction. Daktonian too stood equally stunned.

As two of the riders turned to follow Emma, Raul raised his hand stopping them, and then signaled for them to split and fork out. He himself then gently spurred Daktonian, who began the chase.

The two riders looked at each other perplexed at the sight, then instantly followed Raul's command.

Emma's advantage though not much, gave her enough time to cross the first little hill and disappear from Raul's view. For a second Raul stopped to try and gauge her direction. But he did not have to even wager a guess for in the next instant he heard the jubilant shouts from several men. He followed the sound, glad now of the presence of his two riders for he would surely need their help.

Even before he could see Emma, he knew she was in trouble and probably already their captive. Without stopping, he unsheathed his sword, and rode in the direction of the sounds. As he climbed to the top, he witnessed five men standing around one terrified woman. She was still seated on her palfrey, but even she knew that there was to be no escape for her this time from those men. All they had to do was stretch in her direction and their filthy hands would be on her.

"Did I not tell ye, this wench, would escape again." one man bragged.

"Do ye know what yer master had said, if ye run, I can have the money and ye." Her seller reminded her.

"I might bid for her this time, John, for that knight must have had a reason to bid for her before. Maybe we missed seeing the beauty in her. I will buy myself, a knight's mistress." The third man laughed.

Emma felt sick in the stomach. She recalled the knight's words. "If ye run, I will not follow ye. They will". How foolish she had been not to heed to his warning. Her fate in his hand would undeniably have been better than what these animals planned.

The seller moved his horse closer and his sinister smile sent shivers down Emma's back. As she opened her mouth to scream his filthy hand quickly covered it, killing it to a whimper before her sound could manifest itself into that scream.

"Touch her and ye forfeit yer life! Did ye not hear what I said before?" the roar made all five men turn in Raul's direction.

"Aye Sir, I did hear ye" the seller remarked with sarcasm, "I also heard ye say that if she runs, I could have her and the coins."

"But as ye can see, she is not running, she rides" Raul spoke in an even tone but on noting that Emma was choking under the man's strong grip, added more harshly "Remove yer hands off her at once."

"Sir, the odds are against ye. And the woman is amidst us. Ye would not want our blades to miss their mark, and hurt the wench, now would ye?" The seller challenged.

Raul had feared this moment through the entire journey. Fighting while Emma remained trapped between the men would end the battle but it would also take her life. He gave a quick glance behind the riders and found his prayer answered. His two riders had taken their places. They awaited his signal. Only concern for the woman's safety now prevented their charge.

Deliberating on when they should make that move, he was amazed to see Emma reach towards her waist and produced a dagger, which she plunged into the seller's hand with a swiftness he had only seen on a battlefield. His scream distracted his men and Emma took the moment to jump off the palfrey and swiftly escape through their circle. And then she ran again, surprisingly nimble on her feet. The difference in her running this time was that, she ran not away, but towards Raul.

There was no moment to ponder further. He raced his horse between Emma and the five men who having recovered from their shock, now broke rank, with three coming towards him and the other two circling around towards Emma.

A second later, Raul's two riders, had joined in the fray. Sword met sword, destrier jostled steed. By the time Emma turned to look back, four of the five men that had held her captive moments ago lay dead on the ground. Only the seller remained, and he was still riding towards her. And chasing behind him, was the knight

As the man, reached out for her, hoping to pull her onto his steed, Raul, kicked him off it. The man rose and charged towards Emma, who now was too stunned to move. Frozen in time, she watched, as Raul, dived at the man from his destrier and both men rolled to the ground.

Just then she noticed that the knight's riders had reached her and taken a stand on either side.

"Aid him," she screamed at his riders.

The taller of the two smiled, "Ma'am only one person is going to walk away alive and it is not going to be the one that attacked ye." His words were brave but Emma noticed that neither man had put away his sword.

"Ye are foolish, Sir, to stain ye hand with blood, for a mere wench. If ye want her for yer mistress, keep her for she is not to my liking." the seller goaded.

"Be careful, very carefully how ye speak about a lady." Raul said with a raised voice.

"A lady? Is that the lie she has told ye. She is a maid Sir, a kitchen maid. I had it from a man who travelled in her party." the man yelled.

"And where is the man?" Raul asked.

"Long dead from his wounds, if he be lucky." the seller replied, as he slowly edged towards Emma.

Raul's men moved directly in front of her. Seeing his path blocked, the seller grabbed the dagger tied to his side, and took aim at Emma. In the next instant, Raul's sword had met it's mark.

Emma turned away in horror as blood spurted onto her garment. All her life she had fought against violence. She fought her father against it. She fought her brother against it, even the crusades, she had condemned. And now when she had been moments from death, all she had thought of, prayed for, was the death of the five men. She finally understood, why, man chose to fight. Sometimes, that is the only defense. Sometimes, only violence has the power to end violence.

"I am sorry that ye were forced to witness this." Raul spoke in a gentle tone. But nothing in his tone said, that he was sorry for what he had done.

How was she to respond to his comment, when she had seen worse since she had left home just a few days before? How could she tell him that the man who had died protecting her was not a stranger? That she had been the cause of so much bloodshed in the past and would be the reason for more in the future. And worst of all, she was totally helpless to prevent any of it. Without a man to protect her now, she was an unwilling but available prey for any man that wished to attack.

She had thought the knight weak, when he had bought her instead of fighting for her freedom. She knew now, the man was no coward. He was a strategist. And she was glad that he had not kept his word, and not followed. She prayed hard that their present would not hurt his future, for two who aided her had already come to harm.

When she had not responded to his apology, he continued 'we best get ye inside the castle. Safety lies within those walls. These men will be picked up later and left outside the castle to be claimed by their kin."

Again she climbed onto her palfrey, refusing the help of the knight. The taller of the riders removed her dagger, wiped in on the dead man's clothes and handed it back to her. The act surprised her, for it spoke of trust and she had not expected that. On the ride back, the knight led the party. Her palfrey followed his destrier and his men rode on either side of her, ensuring no attacker could reach her. It had been a long time since she felt so protected. It gladdened her heart yet it also worried her. Why would he risk his life to save her, a mere wench? Was it possible he knew who she was?

The drawbridge must have been raised as soon as they left, for it was being lowered once more.

They rode over its wooden planks and crossed over the moat. Riding under the barbican they entered an open bailey. Raul stopped in front of an arched entrance and alighted. A youth ran forward and took hold of Daktonian's reign and bowing to Raul, led the destrier away, stroking its neck as he walked.

Another, even younger than the boy before, came and stood where the youth had stood earlier.

Raul walked toward Emma's horse. "Do ye need to be assisted?" he asked.

Emma declined the offer, sliding down the side of her palfrey and landing on the ground with a slight thud.

"Marcus will look after yer palfrey" With these words Raul handed the reins to the boy saying "Her name is Athena, see that she remains safe"

The boy led the mare away too but not before giving a curious glance towards Emma. Her dirty garment, now stained with blood did not seem to worry him, but he did wrinkle his nose, as if the smell that surrounded her did.

"Winifred." Raul called to the woman now standing at the top of the stone steps that rose ahead of Emma. "Ready the Tower Room and a bath. When yer lady had finished, escort her back to the great hall where we will have supper."

Turning to Emma he said," Go with Winifred. Ye are safe here, for even I, trust her with my life."

If Emma was surprised to be addressed as 'yer lady', Winifred was even more so. There in front of her stood a woman who was worse dressed than she, yet their Lord has called her 'yer lady' not just 'lady' as he normally referred to the ladies that visited. She noticed too, that the two riders had also raised their eyebrows and exchanged a questioning look.

Dutiful as always, Winifred led Emma away towards the keep and climbed the circular stairwell that seemed to hug the shape of the outer wall. Emma followed silently, awed by the size of the main hall, and impressed by the cleanliness around.

As they went out of view, Raul turned to the two men standing silently, with their questions still written on their faces.

"Thank ye for following. I did not think they would make it this far. For them to be able to guess where we were heading, they must have recognised the insignia on Daktonian. We did not travel the normal paths fearing an attack and I did not see anyone follow."

"Raul! Who is the lady?" The taller one asked as if that was more important than the information Raul had just supplied.

The three called each other by their names, only when they were alone. They had shared much suffering in the past together and had become closer than kin. In public however, the titles and positions came into play.

"My betrothed" Raul replied bereft of any emotion.

"Yer what?" Both men queried together.

"Peter, since when are ye hard of hearing. Emma is the woman I am going to wed." Raul spoke.

"A mere maid? Ye heard what the man said." the second remarked

"A kitchen maid, but she will suit me just fine Rowan. In fact, none would have been better." Raul smiled.

"What happened at yer fathers?" Peter queried.

"My father wishes to see me wed. Nothing has changed much where that is concerned." Raul answered, once again bereft of emotion.

"I heard, there was disagreement." Peter remarked

"How is it, the news has reached before I did?" Raul grinned.

"Ye left yer squire behind when ye left in a rage. Yer father delivered him, just moments ago. We were about to set off with the others, when the guard saw ye both riding in. We worried a mishap had occurred to cause yer delay." Rowan filled in.

"Aye! My father, it is a wonder he did not get the bride delivered as well." Raul scoffed

"I must be getting old, Raul." Peter smiled, "Ye bride is with yer father, yet yer betrothed is here with ye? What brings about this strange situation?"

"We will talk inside. For now, make sure all the guards know, that the lady is not to leave the castle. She is to be kept in sight, always. If she leaves, is taken or if anything happens to her, it will be at the cost of their lives." Raul was stern in his command. He then made his way towards the great hall.

"My Lord!" Sir Rowan called after him.

"What is it Rowan?" Raul inquired

"Does 'our lady' know that she is yer betrothed or have ye forgotten to inform her of it?" The question was serious, but the grin on Sir Rowan's face could not be held back.

Raul was silent a moment and then he said, "She will."

"And does she know, who she is to be betrothed to?" Sir Rowan asked

"She will." he repeated and with that reply he marched inside.

Sir Rowan and Sir Peter, frowned at each other but did not utter a word, instead both dispersed to fulfill Raul's orders.

## Chapter 4

Emma followed Winifred as they climbed the wooden steps. On the first level was another large hall that seemed to be used as a dormitory for the women at night and a work area during the day. Above that level were four smaller rooms. This seemed to be where the women of the castle lived. They crossed the biggest of the rooms with its huge wooden bed in the center. The wooden doors were shut to the next two rooms. Winifred went past them and reached the final room. As she pushed the door, Emma got a glimpse of a room that was smaller than the first. It too had a wooden bed in it but this one had tapestries hanging from the walls making it feminine in nature. The window was open and a clear blue sky was visible.

"This is to be yer room My Lady, I will organise a bath for ye and once it is ready I will come and escort ye there. The bath is near the kitchen. The Baron thought it was more sensible than carrying the water up." Winifred pointed out.

"Ye make a mistake Winifred. This room is not where I should be." Emma remarked.

"No? I was asked to bring ye to the Tower Room. This is the Tower Room, My Lady."

"But I am a mere maid. I have no place in a room such as this." Emma protested.

This news took Winifred by surprise. Was it possible that she was mistaken in her hearing? Why was a servant being given the room of her late mistress?

"If ye remain here my la.., My Lady, I will go and speak with My Lord." Winifred said with uncertainty,

Leaving Emma in the room by herself, Winifred hurried down the tower's steps.

A maid given the Tower Room! That was unheard of, yet her Lord had referred to the woman as 'yer lady' as well. Surely she could not be mistaken on both matters?

As she reached the great hall, she saw her lord walking towards the bailey.

"My Lord!" Winifred chased after him. She had done that for him when he was but a child, she did that still, though he was a man.

"What is it Winifred? Is something the matter, for ye to come in such haste?" he queried

"Nay My Lord, nothing of concern, but the lady upstairs, calls herself a maid and claims there is some mistake in taking her to the Tower Room. Is there My Lord?"

Winifred was the only woman who dared to speak to Raul as she did.

She had gone with Raul's mother to Wilbert when Raul was born. And she had cared for Raul until he was sent as squire. She was there to hold him at the loss of his mother. And she was here to receive him as her next

Baron. She had always known that day would come, for Raul's mother had been an only child. When Raul's grandfather looked to an heir, it was but natural that he would choose his beloved and only grandson.

"No, no mistake in taking her there." Raul turned to walk away.

"And is the lady as she claims, a mere maid, My Lord?" she questioned further.

"That is what I have just been informed." was his only response.

"And My Lord, thinks it is acceptable that a maid be given such honour?" she continued.

"Winifred, while I care not that all know, that she was a maid, I want ye to make sure everyone understands that, she is to be treated as a lady." he was softly firm.

"If she is a mere maid, then with what authority does she become a lady, My Lord?" Winifred continued.

"By the authority of holy matrimony." he clarified.

"Ye plan to wed her. A maid! What can ye be thinking of My Lord? Yer father will never accept this.' Winifred remarked, then suddenly stopped and looked at Raul. "Ah, I see, that is what this is about, isn't it, My Lord? Ye act thus to upset him."

"Ye are too astute, Winifred. No wonder my mother trusted only ye with my life. Aye that is what I plan." Raul replied calmly.

"Ye play a dangerous game My Lord." Winifred worried over the news.

"I have always played a dangerous game. Ye know that of me, by now." This time he grinned.

"Be careful my son, yer father's bride, may not be able to harm ye, she can harm 'yer' lady." She only called him son, when she worried about him, as his mother had done. The last time she had called him that was when he returned wounded after the last battle for his king and she had spent twenty-one nights keeping vigil by his bed, calling on all the saints in heaven and all the herbs on earth, for his healing.

Raul's eyes took on a steely look before he replied "I have assured her of my protection. That protection will keep her safe from my father or his bride."

Winifred was truly worried. She had always been suspicious of her mistress's accident. But Maja had strong connections at the king's court. To have raised questions would have incurred the wrath of the nobility. Raul's father was smitten by the woman and saw no wrong in her. And then, she had no evidence to support her claim, only her feelings.

This marriage, her lord planned would put another mistress' life at risk. For what purpose? Revenge! Like his father, she too would have liked to have seen him married and with his own sons, but his wish had been, to become a Templar Knight.

Had he married because he wanted to, she would have been overjoyed, but to give up one dream, and yet sacrifice another, made no sense. This revenge would only end up hurting Raul. Lord Bruce and his bride would remain unaffected. Her only hope lay in his two closest friends - Sir Rowan and Sir Peter. Maybe they would be able to reason with him and to stop this folly before it was too late.

She left when she realised that she had no more questions. Raul left because he wanted to answer no further.

Next Winifred organised the bath and climbed the stairwell again. This time her ageing legs took longer. When she reached the second level she went towards the room but found the room empty. The door leading to a side rampart was open and her new mistress stood looking out onto the gatehouse from it.

"My Lady!" Winifred spoke and noted that the lady turned to her with a start.

"I have spoken with my lord, and ye are to stay here. There has been no mistake. Yer bath is also ready. If ye would follow me I will direct ye back down. Do ye have another garment to change into My Lady?"

"Whose room is this?" Emma asked, not moving.

"It belonged to my lord's mother" Winifred replied.

"And where is she?" she asked, softly this time

"She was buried, many moons ago" Winifred replied trying hard to sound unaffected.

Emma was in turmoil. Once more she asked herself why would anyone give a mere maid the best room of the keep, especially when she was a stranger and the room had once belonged to the lady of the castle? Only one thing would explain the act. The knight had bought her and now wanted to sell her to his own lord, The Lord of Kinsborough. That is what her guardian had tried to do before he decided he would wed her himself. Now the knight was trying to do the same. Somehow she would have to find a way to leave the keep. Maybe the room with the bath would provide her with the means to escape too. For escape she must.

"My Lady?" Winifred's words broke into the thought.

"What? Oh Aye, bath! I have a garment with me." but to Winifred's surprise, she carried nothing with her when she left the room. An act, that brought another frown to Winifred's brow.

Winifred led Emma back down and to the room with a bath.  As she passed people, Emma noted that they all looked at her oddly, almost as if they too were confused. Maybe they wondered at her relationship with the knight. How could she explain to them that they meant nothing to each other? And that in a short while, would not see each other ever again, but to explain anything would be to jeopardise her escape.

The bath smelled heavenly with its lavender flowers and steaming water. Made from a hollowed tree trunk, it stood two feet tall, three feet long and two feet wide. She has seen a similar one before in London. To empty the bath, one just had to tilt the bath and let the water run out. Emma would have loved the bath, for the water looked so inviting but she had to find a way to escape soon, while not many had seen her and would not question her leaving. Declining help, she requested to be left alone. Winifred promised to be back in a few minutes. She waited some moments to ensure that Winifred was no longer around, then slipped out of the room and retraced her steps until she found herself in the ward. She knew where Athena had been taken and headed in that direction.

As soon as she reached the stables, she darted behind a bale of hay and hid behind it until the two squires left. Athena neighed in recognition. Soon she had Athena free. There was no time to find her saddle, so she decided to ride without it. It would be a hard and uncomfortable ride, but she had done it before too.

She used the pillars and building structures to provide her with the cover she needed until she was near the gatehouse. This was going to be the most difficult part of her escape – sneaking through the draw bridge when it next opened. When the sun went down, the serfs and knights, all returned to the castle, the gates were always opened to allow them in. That was going to be her only opportunity. Escaping with a steed was no easy task but her freedom depended on her success. She had escaped once before using the same ploy. She would have to believe that she would succeed again.

But the sun set too late, and her empty bath was discovered by Winifred when the knight sent her to look in to ensure that Emma had not drowned in the water, for she had taken too long and in a room that was strangely silent.

As soon as the bell rang, Emma knew that her disappearance had been discovered and her attempted escape may fail. The ward and bailey were soon filled with men and women. But stubbornly she remained hidden under the gatehouse.

"Was this gate opened since we returned?" Emma recognised the knight's voice and he made it clear that he was upset. The guards above assured him that it had not.

"Then she cannot have left. Have everyone look for her, but no one is to harm her. Arthur, see if her mare is in the stable." Raul knew that where ever Emma was, she could hear him and he wanted her to know that he was looking.

He also wanted to make sure that she never attempted a foolish escape again, so he roared each command. Did she not realise that this was the only place where she would be safe? Once outside the castle she would be outside of his protection too and again a prey for every man.

Emma looked at Athena. If her last chance to escape was to be successful, she would have to do it without Athena.

She pushed the mare in the direction of the stable then waited until she felt safe to move towards the tower attached to the gatehouse. There were always places to hide in a tower. As a child she had always found the trap doors and escape routes. All castles had at least one other hidden passage out.

The mare in the bailey caused enough commotion and everyone's attention was drawn towards her animal. Emma used the opportunity to enter the tower.

And there seated on the third step, sat the knight, ready and waiting to capture his wayward lady.

Emma froze. When had he entered the tower and how had he known that she was under the gatehouse?

"It seems ye have lost yer way, yer bath awaits ye in the keep." His voice was no longer a roar nor was it gentle.

"I .. I wanted to see Athena before I had a bath. And when she ran, I followed her, then lost my way." she lied.

"Yea I thought that would happen. I will make sure that directions are posted around the castle in the future, so ye do not incur this problem again." His words spoke of convenience, yet his eyes spoke with mirth, and she knew that he was aware of her attempt.

"How did ye know I was here Sir?" She had to ask

"The gate is the only means of escape from this castle. It is but natural ye would head in this direction. My guards had seen ye leave the stable with Athena and that horrible odour ye carry about ye, is the one smell I can pick up anywhere. Tallow, is it not?"

"I will not be sold to yer lord" She blurted in response

"What makes ye think I wish to sell ye?" he queried, looking confused.

"Why else am I being kept in the Tower Room?" was her reply.

"Because, that is the best room in the keep and only the best is offered to those who come to stay." he spoke, still remaining seated.

"Even a mere maid? I do not believe that sir." She remarked

"Especially if she is a maid." was his response

"I do not understand?" She queried

"Go have yer bath, and then we will talk."

Emma walked towards the keep with slow steps. Raul walked a pace behind smiling at her attempt to delay their return. As before, Winifred met her at the entrance but this time her countenance showed sympathy and that worried Emma. If Winifred felt sympathy for her, she must know what the knight had planned. What was to befall her now?

In silence, they entered the room with the bath. Emma noticed that a fresh garment had been placed in the room, despite her earlier claim that she had a garment. This time without being asked, Winifred left her in there alone. But unlike the previous time, she did not leave. Instead she sat on a bench just outside the door and looked away. With that one action, Emma knew that she had lost Winifred's confidence and that no one in the castle would ever trust her again.

Chapter 5

While she completed her bath, Raul met with Sir Peter and Sir Rowan and announced "I want ye both to know that tomorrow I wed."

"Is that not too soon?" they echoed

"She has already tried to leave once." Raul explained.

"Twice! We keep count, Raul." Sir Peter remarked with a twinkle in his eye.

"For what purpose, do ye keep count?" Raul was not amused.

"Rowan and I, wagered on how many times the lady will attempt to escape before ye wed. And if she will succeed in escaping?" Peter enlightened him with his reply.

"She will not escape. She merely fears being forced to wed the Lord of Kinsborough." he replied.

"Then let her go Raul. Maybe that is the wisest step." Peter said seriously.

"She and I will talk tonight. If she agrees to be wed, we wed tomorrow, if she wishes to leave, one of ye can escort her to the Abbey." he said

"Abbey! Ye mean she is on her way to take the vow." Rowan asked in disbelief

"Ye, want to be a Templar Knight and she wants to take the veil. What mockery do ye make of marriage Raul when both of ye seek monastic lives?" Peter asked before Raul could respond to Rowan's query.

Again before Raul could respond he heard Rowan comment "Ye plan on a celibate marriage. That is why ye chose her." Sir Rowan asked

"Aye my friends, this marriage will suit us fine. My father compels me to wed with words of threat. I will wed, but on my terms. My terms are that he can have a bride for his son, but my bride will not give him a grandchild. My father's ultimate dream will remain unfulfilled. And that is something my father will never forgive me for." Raul smiled as he uttered the last words.

"Ye ill use the lady, if ye use her for revenge." Sir Peter remarked

"She will have protection. She will have a title. And she will have a castle. It is more than the maid could ever have dreamed of." Raul explained the benefits, wishing he did not feel the guilt of it.

"Most maids do not have those dreams. They dream of wedded bliss." Sir Rowan remarked.

Raul remained silent.

"Raul! What of yer dream? A wedded man cannot become a Templar Knight." Sir Peter asked.

"Though rare, a wedded man can apply to the order, if his bride gives her permission." Raul replied.

"Ye have planned well Raul, but as a knight, I must defend a woman's honour. I cannot allow ye to force her to wed ye when ye offer her no future." Sir Peter stressed.

"I will not force her to wed me. If she agrees to wed me of her own free will, will that satisfy yer code of chivalry?" Raul questioned.

"If she walks to the altar, accepting yer offer, of her own free will, I will be accepting of both of yer choices. Before ye follow through with ye plan, think this Raul, yer plan does not account for the human heart. What if either of ye want differently after ye both are wed?" Peter questioned

"The marriage will be annulled to allow the heart that wants differently to find happiness." Raul remained calm

"I still do not like yer plan, but ye have always been the clever strategist, Raul, and as yer friend, I will be accepting of it, with but, that one condition. She must first agree to wed ye and arrives at the chapel of her own free will." Sir Peter said.

Peter could not understand how Raul could be taking such a risk. Peter had already applied to the Order, and now he awaited the word of acceptance from the Order of the Templar. Maybe that had been the difference between Raul and him. He would never have risked being declined, not for anyone. Yet Raul's path seemed inundated with obstacles -first his father's objection, then his grandfather's need of him, and finally this farcical marriage. One reason or another seemed to always delay his decision. With this marriage, he was jeopardising his chances of every being allowed into the Order. Maybe fate was choosing Raul's path for him and maybe that path did not include becoming a Templar Knight. Rather, it included a bride.

While the men conversed, Emma washed her garments in the pail that had been provided. All five garments! Not wanting to carry a bundle that would hinder her escape, she had left home wearing five garments, one over the other. To ensure her safety she had greased her hair with that abhorrent tallow, suffocating under its odour but preferring it repellant property, for it promised a measure of security.

Once Emma had finished her bath, and had dressed into the garment that had been provided, she looked at her reflection in the bath water.

It would not do. She must not look as she was reflected. The garment was loose which suited her perfectly but the black soot had washed off and her long waist length brown hair was shining and clean, her alabaster skin was gleaming and she smelled of lavender. This look would undo all her efforts. She knew she must return to looking as she had done before.

She asked Winifred for a lamp, with the excuse that she needed more light. She asked for a wrap saying she was cold. Alerted by her earlier attempt, Winifred left another maid as guard and went to clear these requests with her lord. When Winifred returned with the items, Emma let out a sigh of relief.

She replaced the lamp and taking the old one, she scraped out the grease and soot and massaged it into her hair. Then she tightly knotted her hair into an untidy bun that rested on the nape of her neck. Finally she applied the soot to her face. Covering herself with the wrap she walked out and saw disappointment on Winifred's face. While the odour no longer existed, the lady looked almost as she had when she arrived. Dirty, greasy and very plain!

Winifred sent the other maid, whom she addressed as Mary, to empty the bath water and to hang Emma's washed clothes out to dry. She wondered, but did not comment on seeing five garments washed and placed in a pile by the stone bench. She would find out later.

Then she led Emma to the great hall. As she led her, Winifred, felt as a butcher would feel when leading a lamb to its slaughter. As they entered the great hall, Sir Peter and Sir Rowan both stood in respect. A frown appeared on Emma's brow at this act. She was a kitchen maid to them, yet they honoured her as a lady. It raised the question, why?

At that very instant the knight too walked in. Freshly washed and adorning clean garments, without mail or armour, he looked different. He too bowed. Another frown appeared on Emma's brow. All this respect did not bore well.

Then he smiled. Until that moment she had not noticed how handsome he looked. His eyes had lit up with the smile, making him look younger, more human like and praise worthy. She curtsied to him in return but did not otherwise respond to the smile.

"Sir Rowan and I will wash and return shortly. I understand supper is sometime away." Sir Peter was the first to speak.

"Aye, take yer time. I need to speak with the lady." Raul replied.

When they had left and Winifred too had vacated the hall, Raul gestured for Emma to take a seat.

Her countenance had not escaped him. She looked unwashed, but at least the odour was no longer there. Or rather the smell of oil had replaced the smell of tallow.

"I wish to make a request" he stated

"Of me, Sir?" Emma could not understand what a knight could want of her.

"I need a bride" he said without a prelude

At these words, Emma stood and moved towards the door in an attempt to exit the room.

"If ye would but listen to me, ye would realise that what I ask, is the solution to both our problems." he rushed with his words.

"I have no problem sir, except to find a way to reach the Abbey. Marriage sir, will not solve that problem. And ye sir, assured me that ye did not need a mistress or a maid. It was a lie then sir? She questioned, secretly worried at her loss of confidence in him.

"I said I do not need a mistress or a maid, but I never said that I did not need a bride. I do not need the first two, it is the third that I need.  Ye will agree that I said no lie." He countered.

"No sir, ye use words to confuse people. As ye did with the seller, Ye said I was not running, I was riding. I saw no difference in those two acts" she reminded him of the earlier event.

"Ye were on yer mare, and not on yer feet. That is the difference.  I also said I did not need a mistress or a maid, a bride is neither of these" Raul replied.

"A bride should be of one's own kind Sir. A knight may not marry a kitchen -maid, nor a maid a knight." Emma advised.

"I do not believe that such thought is governed by law." he replied.

"No Sir, but that thought is governed by our King and the lords, and both have the power to excommunicate ye from yer kind." she reminded him.

"It is a risk that I am willing to take." Raul remarked calmly.

"But it is a risk I will not, sir." came Emma's reply.

"Yer only objection should have been that ye wish to take the veil, yet that was not yer first thought, why?" he questioned ignoring her reply.

"To stop at the Abbey was my father's request sir; it is not my final destination."

"Where is yer final destination then?" he questioned.

"I cannot say. That information is to be given to me at the Abbey, Sir." was her honest reply.

"Ye take a lot of risk travelling alone on a journey that promises no answers." he added

"I have no other choice sir. If I am to find answers, then I must travel in the direction where they lie." She philosophised.

"But, ye do have another choice. Wed me." Raul offered

"Marriage is not for me sir." Emma remained adamant.

"It is not for me either, yet I am placed in a position where I must wed, or see all that I love, destroyed before my very eyes. It is my father's threat that I marry or he will make his bride's nephew his heir." he explained, knowing that he would have to tell her part of the truth.

That intrigued Emma. "Yer father's bride is not yer mother then?" she queried.

"Nay, my mother died when I was still a child. My father remarried soon after. The woman he married had been his mistress. The woman is known by the name Maja. Unfortunately I still remain his only child. And he now wishes of me the one thing he cannot fulfill without me, the continuation of his name. And so he wants me wed." Raul elaborated.

"Then it is best ye wed someone who will be able to fulfill that task sir. It cannot be done by me. I chose to live a solitary life." came Emma's adamant reply.

"A solitary life or a single life promised to the Lord?" he queried.

"Again ye play with words sir. They are the same." she responded

"Nay again, they differ. A solitary life can be led within the vows of marriage. A promised life is a single one within the vows of the church." he distinguished.

"I do not understand sir." Emma was confused.

"I need a bride, but not a wedded life. Ye want a solitary life but seem not to promise yerself to the Church. Wedding each other would be the answer to both our problems. As my wedded bride, ye will have my protection and a home in this castle yet ye will be free to lead a life of yer own with no demands from me." he said.

This last promise made his offer interesting. Was it possible she was being offered a way to safety and security? This could truly be the answer to her problems. She was not vowed to the church. She was to get information there. Her journey beyond that next step was uncharted for her. His offer was mapping that future for her. It was also offering a safe haven where she could remain hidden and free.

"Why would a man wed, if he was not interested in a wedded life?" she had to ask.

"I pledged myself to a woman once, who is now married to another and I have no desire to follow in that path again." He replied.

"Then, is what ye say true? That ye will make no demands? She whispered

Raul could see the change in her tone. She was looking at his offer. All he had to do was give his assurance, and he would have found himself a bride.

"As long as ye do not leave this castle, I will make no demand. Ye will be safe with yer husband's name and yet ye can remain free of yer husband's company." he promised.

Emma thought a moment. He was a man who was good with his words. Did he offer her a double edged sword or was his offer truly a protective shield?

"To whom sir, am I going to be wed?" came her acceptance. Raul sighed in relief. He had gambled and he had won.

"Baron Raul of Kinsborough, grandson of Late Baron William of Kinsborough and only son of Lord Bruce of Wilbert, My Lady" with that he bowed.

Emma was stunned by the introduction. She would marry a Baron. Surely no lord could hurt her now? She would have the protection of a Baron and of his knights.

"And ye, what name follows Emma?" Emma thought a moment. Her true name must not be revealed. But if they were to marry, she must give him a name that was still true. After a moment's hesitation she replied "Emma of Rosemund, My Lord". With that, she curtsied.

Sir Anthony of Rosemund, was the name her father used when he was on his secret missions to keep his identity hidden. And when she was with her father, he would introduce her as Emma of Rosemund. Only her father and she knew, that Rosemund was not a place, rather it had been the code name of his first mission.

Chapter 6

When before supper, Raul introduced her as his betrothed and she did not object, both Sir Peter and Sir Rowan heaved a sigh of relief. They looked at their new lady, and saw relief written on her face too. That was a good sign.

When next Raul bowed in front of her and kissed her hand, his people cheered. Whether they approved of a maid marrying their lord, Emma, did not know, but she knew this, that their loyalty to their lord was unquestionable and had he married a mule, his people would have accepted it. She would do well to remember this unquestionable loyalty they had for their lord.

Winifred led her to the main table, and she found herself seated to the right of Raul. On his left sat Sir Peter. Sir Rowan sat to her right. A seat remained vacant next to him and was to be left vacant for the Friar who, she was told was attending to a sick serf and would join them shortly.

Supper was a generous meal. Freshly baked warm bread served with soft cheese. Honey mead was served for drink. Apples and peaches were laid on the table for sweet, and large platters of meat from a recent kill was carried by the kitchen hands and served to all. Emma accepted some bread and cheese but declined the meat.

"Ye must eat some. It is needed for nourishment." Raul said on noting the contents of her platter.

"It does not agree with me My Lord" she replied.

"Then what do ye eat?" he inquired

"Vegetables, cheese, bread and fruits My Lord. And some poultry" she replied describing her diet.

"Winifred, please instruct the cook, that poultry and vegetables must be served at every supper for my lady." he addressed Winifred who was seated at the end of the table.

No one had done that for her before. Even her father had mocked her preference. If meat was served, she generally made do with only bread and cheese. Now a stranger looked to her comfort. It made her heart glad. A feeling she had never had before and could not understand even now.

During supper the knights spoke to their lord on various topics. The weather was of most importance for it dictated their daily routine. The land was spoken of with reverence, for it gave them the sense of belonging. Then they delighted in hearing of the gossip from the court. On this night the last conversation turned to the wedding. At that very moment a man walked in dressed in a friar's brown garment.

"My Lord, I have only just returned back and am told I am to perform a wedding on the 'morrow. Yer wedding, My Lord" he spoke in a musical voice almost as if he was singing in a chapel.

"Aye Friar Joseph, there is need for haste" Raul replied. Silence fell in the hall as all tried to partake of the conversation. It was however, the Friar's reaction that angered Raul and humiliated Emma. His eyes fell to her stomach, which covered in a large wrap, looked suspiciously concealed

"And My Lady, is it yer wish to be wed too?" He directed the question to her.

Raul, Peter and Rowan held their breath as Emma hesitated in her answer. And then with her voice almost a whisper, replied "I believe my lord had decided well" All three men again sighed in relief.

"In that case My Lord, My Lady, I wish ye both well." The friar said taking his seat.

People returned to eating, the men to their conversation and Emma, wondered why she had just entrusted her life in the hands of the Baron, when she had not trusted her own kin.

When everyone was busy conversing with each other, Raul turned to Emma and remarked in a hushed voice "I notice, ye play with words too. That was well said."

Emma looked at Raul who was smiling at her and then whispered back "It is an ability I learnt of late, from one ye are well acquainted with."

Raul raised an eyebrow in query and she continued "The Baron of Kinsborough, do ye not know him?" Raul noted that her eyes actually twinkled at her words.

Raul, burst out laughing. Everyone at the table ceased their chatter, and looked at their Lord. It was the first time that many had heard him truly laugh. Winifred was the only one, who remembered that sound from years ago.

After supper, while the men went to walk on the rampart, which Emma learnt was a daily ritual; Winifred escorted Emma to her room. There she found that a dowry box had been placed while she had been away.

"My Lord has directed that we go through this box. It is to be yers My Lady, and ye are to choose whatever ye wish to keep. It belonged to my late mistress. There is a white gown that she wore after my lord's birth. Jane is good with the needle. She and I will alter it tonight if ye wish."

"Is that necessary? My garments will dry by the morrow." Emma queried

"But My Lady, they are old and drab. It is yer wedding day, My Lady, ye should look like a bride. Others will come from My Lord's manors to witness the wedding." said Winifred.

"And is the Lord of Wilbert, coming?" Emma asked, fearful of a positive reply.

"Nay!" At that sound both Emma and Winifred turned to see Raul standing at the doorway. He had not entered the room.

"I am sorry My Lord, I was just curious." Emma replied

"Ye will meet my father in good time, once we are wed. But our meetings will always be infrequent and of brief duration." he added

Winifred made to leave the room, but Raul stalled her.

"Nay, stay with yer lady and help her dress now. We wed in an hour." He announced.

"In an hour! But it will be dark soon." Winifred spoke while Emma looked on stunned.

"I am sorry My Lady, that ye will not have the wedding ye would desire, but it seems my father sent an escort to deliver my squire. That man disappeared after our wedding was announced. I have no doubt, if we do not wed now, we will have a few unwanted guests tomorrow." he informed.

"My Lord! Ye displease a powerful man when ye wed, be it today or tomorrow. But if ye delay yer nuptials, many will risk their life when they stand to defend their lords." Winifred voiced her worry.

"I am, aware of that." Raul replied somberly.

"If I leave My Lord, this will not happen." Emma spoke up.

"Do ye think yer departure from here is going to spare ye from their wrath? The more defenseless a woman is, the more powerful it makes them feel. Without the protection of Kinsborough, ye stand not a chance in hell, My Lady." Raul replied unable to keep the anger out of it.

"So ye fear yer father?" she queried.

"Nay My Lady, I distrust his methods" he replied." Had I feared him, I would have married the woman of his choice."

"Yet ye marry a woman, still not of yer choice, how is it any better?" she asked.

"It is the preferable choice. Our marriage offers ye security. It offers me freedom. I no longer wish to do my father's bidding. It is time I follow my own."

Winifred feeling an appendage to the conversation, tried to leave the room with the words, "I had better go and get the hall ready. Is the Friar already aware of yer intent, My Lord?"

'Yes, he was the first to begin preparation. Arrangements below are managed well, ye best stay with yer lady." Raul replied.

"I will help my lady prepare for the wedding then, but I see the lines of worry on yer brow My Lord. Ye anticipate trouble?" Winifred remarked.

"As always, ye are very astute. Remain with yer lady at all times. The guards are to remain by yer sides as well." Raul informed

Emma wondered at this precaution.

"We are within the castle walls, and if ye could prevent me getting out, surely ye can prevent someone getting in." she asked, playfully mocking his power.

Raul's lips twitched into a faint smile before he replied.

"My Lady, my father's man was not seen leaving. It is presumed he left but it is possible he still remains. At all times ye must remain in sight of Sir Peter, Sir Rowan or yer betrothed. And if I send ye any message, it will be through Winifred. Winifred alone! Do not heed, that from any other." he cautioned

"My Lord, ye plan as if we go to battle!" Emma commented.

"Nay My Lady, the battle began many years ago, at the death of my mother. We go to end that battle." he declared.

Emma frowned. She longed to ask what he meant by it, but Raul had already backed away from the door.

"Make haste, I would have the marriage over with soon." were Raul's last words before he was gone. Not down to the halls as she would have thought, but in the direction of his own room. She could see his squire wait inside the door.

"My Lady, there is no time to wash out the soot and grease from yer hair, nor to scrub ye clean with another bath. The best that can be done is to wipe the grease off and wash ye face with lavender water"

"How did ye know? I mean about my hair." Emma asked

"Because when I went to the room, My Lady, the lamp was wiped clean, the black grease was gone, and yer freshly washed hair, was covered in it. I know My Lady, that ye must have yer own reason to wish to hide it, but even with the grease, its beauty cannot be hidden."

Emma smiled at the irony of Winifred's comment. But Winifred was right, she had taken the steps she thought were needed, for she was a woman travelling alone, not knowing who among those she met, would be her enemies. Who among those she met, would wish her harm!

Winifred helped Emma get ready. There was no time to take in the dress, so they did the best they could by binding it tight, with twines. Raul's old baby coverlet was used as a veil. His mother's girdle was tied loosely around her waist giving it shape for the first time since her arrival.

"My Lady, when ye first came ye seemed larger and I thought my lady's garment would be too small, yet now we had to bind ye in twine to keep the garment in place. How is it that ye become thinner with but one bath?" Winifred asked wondering how Emma had managed to hide her slimmer figure.

"I wore many garments at once so I would not have to carry them while travelling." Emma remarked knowing that the reason she gave was only partly true.

"Ye mean ye wore the five garments that ye washed My Lady, all at once?" Winifred was astounded.

"Yea and more." Emma smiled.

"Well the Friar at least will be relieved. He thought ye were with child." Winifred confirmed Emma's own thought.

"I too saw his gaze move to my stomach. For a Friar, he assumed much." Emma remarked.

"He but judges harshly, for Lord Wilbert, married in haste because his second bride was with child when they wed." Winifred added.

"I know my lord does not have a brother, then he must have a half-sister?" Emma asked in surprise.

"Nay My Lady, the child died. Maja went to her parent's home when it was time for the babe to be born, but when Lord Bruce reached soon after the birth it was to find out that babe had died in the womb and was birthed dead. The babe lies buried at her parent's manor. The Friar may have seen the Baron's rush to marry, as a repeat of what happened before."

"Ah, I understand better now. I will no longer think him impolite for assuming the worst of me" Emma replied.

"The Friar is a holy man, with a good heart My Lady. Sometimes he just forgets that a good heart and a soft tongue should go together." Winifred vouched.

"I will remember that, when he next finds fault with me." Emma laughed. Winifred joined in.

When at the next instant they heard a knock on the door Winifred replied without a query, "We are ready and we follow ye My Lord"

Winifred held back until the sound of Raul's footstep had ceased and then she opened the door. Mary stood beside the guards, ready to assist. Together they guided Emma down the stairwell and out into the ward. Children had gathered at the entrance and peered to get a glimpse of the Baron's bride. Women 'oohed' and aahed' and followed Emma as they made their way to the porch outside the chapel just yards away.

As they neared the porch, someone started a low hum. A hauntingly beautiful melody, that brought an ache to Emma's heart and a tear to her eye. Winifred handed her a piece of cloth to wipe away the tear, as she gently squeezed her arm. Then they made their way through a floral arch, made from wild rose creepers growing over a wooden frame. On the other side of the arch, a knight stood with a bunch of flowers. He smiled as she reached him, and she recognised him as Sir Peter. Had he not smiled, dressed as he was in chain mail she would have passed by him.

Now he handed her the bouquet made up the same wild roses and surrounded by the leaves of Rosemary, as he uttered the words, "These are from the Baron My Lady. I have also been charged to give ye my lord's message 'the roses are to honour yer past home, the rosemary to remind ye of yer future one".

At first she looked at the bunch in confusion, until she remembered that she had told Raul, that, she was from Rosemund. Most places that had the name Rose or Rosa as part of their names were usually renowned for their beautiful wild roses. For a warrior, to think such a thought made him sound human.

"Thank ye Sir Peter. I am unlikely to ever forget, Kinsborough, its Baron, or the honour he does me." She replied with sincerity.

"Then My Lady, I take it that ye walk to the altar of yer own free will?" Peter asked.

When Emma nodded in response, he continued, "In that case, My Lady, may I be the first to offer my felicitation!" With the end of those words, he bowed in front of Emma.

"Thank ye Sir Peter, I pray I am not late, my lord, desired, that there be no delay" she replied with a smile.

At this, Sir Peter looked towards Raul, who was not looking pleased as all. Peter smiled back.

"Yea My Lady, the once reluctant groom, seems anxious to be wed." he joked.

"Tell me Sir Peter, does yer friend live his life by hasty decisions and reckless actions?" she jested back.

"Nay My Lady, he does not have the liberty of indulging in either. Too many lives depend on him" Peter replied, loyalty breathing through his words.

"Yet, he weds me!" With that Emma continued her walk towards the Friar. Peter looked quizzingly at Raul, before racing after Emma, having momentarily forgotten that he had been assigned to give the bride away. As he had already taken on the role of her protector, Raul had assigned this duty to him as well.

"My Lady, I believe I am to give ye away". Peter spoke.

Emma stopped until Sir Peter caught up to her, then laid her palm on his hand, and silently continued on her march to the porch.

Friar Joseph, too, was glad to see Emma approach unshackled, and was strangely pleased at the sight of Sir Peter chasing the bride. It bode well that the bride too was keen to exchange the vows.

As Emma reached the Friar, she turned for the first time to look at her betrothed and froze at the sight of Raul in his full battle gear. The knight she had agreed to marry had been replaced by a warrior she did not know. Dressed in chain mail from head to heel, his sword lay sheathed at his waist. Over thick trousers, he wore leather stockings. From shoulder to knee he wore a hauberk. Above that he wore a Ventail and an Aventail that covered his face, neck and shoulders. Yet over all of this, he wore a red surcoat with the insignia of a white lion.  Sir Rowan stood beside him, holding Raul's spangenhelm and shield. The shield also had the same insignia. The very one she had seen on Daktonian's saddle.

Momentarily she hesitated. A warrior husband! Could she live the rest of her life amidst wars and battle cries, loss and pain?

"Are ye well, My Lady?" Raul asked with concern. The sight of a battle ready knight brought comfort to most women, but Emma seemed frightened by him. He saw the hesitation in her action. He saw the fear in the look she cast over him.

"My Lord, we really do go to battle" she remarked. With that she looked around to find that even his knights were dressed as though prepared to defend.

"Nay My Lady, we stand in readiness. Ye tarried long in yer conversation with Sir Peter. Every moment we now delay endangers my men" Raul reinforced, clearly not pleased with her stop.

"If ye wish to avoid any delay, mayhaps next time, it would be best ye give the bouquet and the message, yerself My Lord". The smile she gave him through the veil, left Raul speechless, the Friar pleased and Peter and Rowan grinning. No woman had dared to reprimand Raul as such before.

While Raul stood staring at her, Emma took her place before the Friar and bowed her head as if in prayer.

Raul followed suit. A moment later, Friar Joseph began the rites with the words

"I need that if either of ye know any impediment, why ye may not be lawfully joined together in matrimony, that ye confess it now.  For ye be guaranteed, that so many as be wed together otherwise than God's Word doth allow are not joined together by God; neither is their matrimony lawful"

For a second both Emma and Raul looked at each other. Raul had not told her why he was truly marrying 'her' and she had not told him who 'she' really was. Yet this marriage suited both and was the best for both their futures. How could that be wrong in the eyes of God?

There was not a sound apart from the friar's voice as he sang the verses. Emma heard the melody in his words. She knew her name was taken. She heard Raul's name too. A half hour later the Friar asked for the rings to be blessed. Two golden rings were placed in the Friars hand. After they were blessed, they were given back to the couple to exchange. Emma wondered how Raul had managed to organise the ring so soon. She would learn later that hers had belonged to Raul's mother.

"With this ring, I thee wed." Raul's words sealed her fate.

When Raul raised her hand to seal their union, with the customary kiss, Emma responded as she curtsied to just the right height. In that instant Raul knew that Emma would have had to have been much closer to her mistress than she had claimed, for no kitchen maid would have known the correct protocol required of a lady.

After this the friar asked them to sign the register, Raul signed his name first and then passed the quill to Emma. She looked at his name, hesitated only a moment and then signed it simply as Emma. She had pondered over the dilemma as she walked to the church. She could have signed it as Emma of Rosemund, but while it would be true for the people it would not be true for her God.

Standing in His house, she had no option but to sign it as Emma for that at least for partly true.

Instead of giving it back to Raul she handed it back to the Friar. The Friar waved the document to ensure that the ink had dried and then he rolled up the parchment and tied it with twine. This he handed to Raul. When Raul did not undo the twine, the fear in Emma abated. What would the Baron do, if he knew, who he had just wed?

Chapter 7

Their marriage was celebrated with music, dancing and a feast. Poultry was served for her while wild boar and venison was served to the others.

The crowd called for the bridal couple to dance. As the cheering grew, a knight rushed into the great hall, requesting to speak to the Baron alone. Raul and the man disappeared into the ward. When Raul next returned, it was to announce that the festivities would have to be delayed. They would have visitors soon, but it was not yet certain if those that rode towards the castle were friends or foe. Emma noted that his words were instantly met with the action of his knights arming themselves.

Raul then walked to Emma.

"My Lord, how is it that ye do not know if they are friend or foe? Surely they carry their flag and insignia?" Emma asked as he reached her side.

"The insignia is that of my father. It remains to be seen if he comes as friend or foe." was Raul's reply.

"My Lord, whatever ye relationship be with him, he is still yer father. Let now the first arrow be released from Kinsborough." she pleaded.

Raul looked at his bride.

"Is that the wedding gift ye ask, My Lady? The safety of my father and his men over the safety of ye husband and his?" he queried.

"Nay My Lord, I ask for the safety of yer father at the cost of the safety of yer bride" she replied.

Three vertical lines appeared between his brows, as Raul, puzzled over her reply.

"My Lord, I offer to stand in place of yer knights." she replied

A hush fell in the great hall. His bride had offered to take an arrow for his men. A moment of silence was soon followed by the sound of armour moving as knight after knight went down on one knee in homage. The ladies followed their men and curtsied.

Winifred watched with pride as Emma, without realising it herself, had truly made herself the new Lady of Kinsborough. Misty eyed she smiled at this happy result.

Raul took in the scene before him too. Only one other lady had ever been given this reverence. That lady had been his mother. When he looked at Emma, her eyes too floated with unshed tears at the sight in front of her.

"My Lady, we did not wed, so ye could exit our marriage so soon." Raul spoke in a hushed tone with only those at their table hearing his words. The rest knew their lord's words were personal, for their lady had finally blushed.

Aloud he said "My father is to be treated as an honoured visitor. Sir Peter and Winifred will remain with my lady. Sir Rowan and I will ride out to meet my father as soon as we are assured; it is him that rides our way. Within the castle all are to remain alert. If there is an attack on us, the gates are not to be opened. Kinsborough must be kept safe. And my lady, is not to be surrendered at any cost. I ask this of all of ye."

Emma rose from the table as he ended his words.

"My Lord, I seek permission to ride with ye" Emma pleaded.

"It cannot be given. Ye are to remain here under Sir Peter's care. My father is not the only one that rides. With him are many known to Ma'am and who would do her bidding." He replied.

"Then stand within and permit only yer father to come through, My Lord" Emma pleaded.

Raul looked at his bride. Was she worried about him? Surely not, for they had been acquainted for less than a day.

"That would pronounce me, a coward. I am not afraid of him and I will not allow him to think I am." Raul replied.

"Then take me with ye. For having a bride of yer choice by yer side will truly prove, that ye are not afraid of the Lord of Wilbert." Emma challenged. Had she issued that when they were alone he might have scoffed or laughed at it. But her challenge had been made in public and by the look in her eyes; she knew that she had played a clever hand, one that she knew she would win.

Raul looked at Sir Peter, who though still anxious, now openly smiled. Emma not waiting for his reply turned to ask Winifred for a wrap. The decision it seemed had been made for Raul and strangely for the first time Raul did not mind it. But before Emma left his side, he stopped her.

"My Lady, that was again, cleverly done. My father however is not as obliging as me, it would be wise that ye do not play the same hand with him." he uttered.

"Ah My Lord, the secret is to only play with the top cards of a deck. It matters not then, who it is that ye play with." With the first real smile at him since their acquaintance, Emma moved towards Winifred who had just returned with the wrap. And though Emma had turned away from him, her impish smile, her twinkling eyes and her glowing cheeks remained imprinted in Raul's vision. How, had he ever thought her plain? There was beauty there that until now had somehow gone unnoticed.

"My Lord, it appears a mere maid, has just bested the Baron of Kinsborough" Peter remarked.

"Aye, it appears as that." Raul smiled back.

With that, both Raul and Peter put on their spangenhelms and picked up their swords. The knights that had been in the hall had already rushed out to ready themselves.

"My Lady, the Baron speaks wisely when he says, that many may ride with the Lord of Wilbert, who would do ye harm. Ye will be careful will ye not? It would also be a foolish time to attempt another escape" Winifred whispered to Emma as they walked towards her palfrey.

"Winifred, fear not, I merely go to ensure that the man I wed today does not make me a widow this night." Emma replied.

"And ye will not attempt to escape?" Winifred asked again.

"I am wed now Winifred. I am bound by oath. It is true I did not wish to be a bride, but it is also true, I wish not to be left alone." Emma eased away the fear in Winifred.

"Ye have been wed, but a few hours, and ye already doubt yer husband's strength." Raul's words broke through, confirming that he had overheard their conversation.

"I doubt not my husband's strength My Lord, but as ye said, yer Ma'am has many who would do her bidding." she answered

"And ye believe an unarmed woman, can save a man from their weapons?" he asked

"Nay My Lord, I believe a bride can save her husband from their misconception." she replied.

"Come then My Lady, the Lord of Wilbert could well do with a dose of yer arguments." Raul laughed. Emma frowned. Sir Peter smiled and Winifred looked utterly confused.

Chapter 8

Mere hours after she had entered the gate as the Baron's maid, she rode through it now as his bride. Once it was ascertained that Lord Bruce rode himself and came with only his friend Maximillian and a handful of knights, Raul reduced the number of his own knights that rode out with him, leaving more to protect the castle.

The meeting of father and son was just as Raul had predicted to her before their marriage. Cordial in greeting and even more cordial in exchange! To say that Lord Bruce was surprised to see Emma by Raul's side was an understatement. That she was beneath him was made obvious to all when there was no smile for her, nor an acknowledgement as she bowed seated on Athena.

"Ye are wed?" he asked of his son.

"Father, this is Emma, my bride of some hours." Raul replied.

"What jest do ye play with me son? Yesterday ye wished not to wed, today ye present me with a bride." his father screamed.

"Father, yesterday ye gave me an ultimatum, wed or lose Wilbert. Today I fulfilled yer demand. I am wed and here is my bride." Raul replied.

"Is it not customary to have yer father at yer wedding?" Lord Bruce asked, continuing to ignore Emma.

"I do not remember being invited to yers. Our circumstance was unusual, it was important we wed quickly." Raul answered

"Ye were too young to attend mine. What circumstances would yers be, save to vex me further or do ye tell me she already carries yer child?" Lord Bruce questioned further, and added insult to his question. An insult he directed at Emma while still ignoring her.

"I lost once before because I tarried long, I feared my second would also leave if I delayed further." Raul replied, though his reply made Emma turn and look at her husband trying to judge her husband's emotions as he uttered those words.

"That girl was unsuitable then. This woman is unsuitable now." Lord Bruce raised his voice as he uttered the words.

"Suitability and beauty have much in common father. Only the beholder knows of its value." Raul replied

"Ye chose a mason's daughter the last time. I hear, ye do not even know whose daughter ye have chosen this time. That makes this one more unsuitable than the last. And I see no beauty in her?" the father taunted the son.

"It matters not who fathered my bride. It matters only that no one else fathers her child." Raul was still calm

"Had ye declared yer desire to wed such common blood, my current mason also had an unwed daughter" his father's angry words were loud enough for the guards on the barbican to hear.

"I am surprised that under yer care she remains unwed. What happened father, are ye not as powerful anymore? It must be hard losing yer control over yer people's lives?" Raul's insulting words shocked both Lord Bruce and Emma, silencing his father for a moment.

"My Lords!" Emma began

"This is betwixt my son and me ma'am." Lord Bruce cut her short.

"Not when it is me ye both fight over, My Lord." Emma replied looking confidently at Lord Bruce. Only Raul knew she was shaking inside as he noted her quivering fingers.

"Well! Well! I must say ye do surprise me. At least Rosalie knew her place. She did not speak when she was not spoken to." Bruce burst out

"Much good that did her My Lord, for it is I who stand by yer son as his bride." Emma responded. Raul could not help but smile.

"Insubordinate woman, for ye my son has ruined his family?" he unjustly charged.

"I am unable to accept the blame for that My Lord, if yer family is ruined; it was done before I arrived. My acquaintance with yer son is of much shorter duration." by now Emma's legs too were shaking. Luckily she was seated atop Athena and it did not show to those mounted.

"Ye may not have done the damage, but ye can undo it." Bruce added.

"I do not understand My Lord?" Emma replied.

"Annul the marriage. Ye are newlywed, it can be easily got." Bruce suggested.

"Father! It is best ye do not request of Emma that which is not within her power to give." Raul cut it.

"Then ye request for it. It is within yer power, is it not?" Bruce argued.

"Yea father I have 'that' power, but I do not have 'that' wish" Raul replied then continued "It would be wise if we speak inside the keep. Ye are welcome.." Raul's invitation was rejected even before it was completed.

"I have seen what I came to see. My son, Baron of Kinsborough and heir of Wilbert, standing beside the whore he married" With these word, Bruce insulted both his son and his son's bride.

"FATHER!" Raul had drawn his sword. Within seconds swords were drawn by all.

"My Lord, please!" Emma addressed Raul "It matters not what I am called, for I have been called worse before. It matters only that no sword is raised on my account, especially by a son against his father." Emma pleaded

"I do not need ye to plead my case." Lord Wilbert screamed at Emma

"I do not plead yer case My Lord, I plead mine." Emma replied looking at Raul as she spoke without even a glance at Lord Wilbert.

And then everyone watched with disbelief, as Raul, lowered his sword arm. An air of relief spread over all.

"Lord Bruce, it might be wise to return now". Maximillian cut in. He had accompanied Bruce as a friend. No matter what the lady's past had been, as Raul's bride she now deserved the respect the title gave her. It was the courtesy they had all given Lord Bruce's wives, even Maja. Raul's mother had been a much respected lady, admired and loved by all. To see Maja in her role was not easy to accept for many, not possible to accept for Raul, yet it was what all did for Lord Bruce's sake. And now when it was his turn to extend that same respect to his son's bride, Lord Bruce had been unable to do so. To see his friend, a brave knight himself, attack the lady's integrity in such a dishonourable way, did not conform to the code of chivalry.

"Let's go Maximillian; I have seen what there was to see. Maja was right once again, my son's purpose in life is to destroy my good name." Without another word, he turned his steed and rode away. Maximillian followed him, though before leaving he bowed his head in a farewell to both Raul and Emma. The remaining members of his party also rode away, surprisingly, they too did the same.

Emma stared after Lord Bruce. That had not gone well at all. And then she looked at Raul to see his reaction. He was not looking at his father; instead, his eyes were set on her. Emma gave him a sad smile, before she said,

"Ye did wrong My Lord, in marrying me. Ye did worse, by not inviting yer father."

"Ye defend my father, after all that he uttered?" Raul asked in amazement.

"My Lord, yer father speaks from anger and hurt. It is not him that I defend. It is him that I pity. If ye had a son, who wed without yer presence, to a woman ye did not like, would ye not react in a similar manner?" Emma asked.

"My relationship with my son would have been different." was Raul's reply. But as his father rode away Raul experienced regret, that he would never experience a relationship with a son, good or bad. For the first time, that was felt with pain.

"More so to pity him for, My Lord, more so to pity him!" Emma concluded.

As they rode back into the castle, Raul leaned over towards Emma and asked,

"Ye insisted on coming with us, pray tell me, what misconception were ye able to clear up with yer presence here?" His words were filled with mirth.

"That ye had fallen in love with a beautiful wealthy woman, who had become the second great love of yer life, and who carried the future heir to both Wilbert and Kingsborough. That misconception, if it ever existed has been cleared forever, My Lord." she replied.

Raul read the sadness that had once again been reflected in those words. But more than that, he remembered

Peter's words, "Ye ill use her if ye use her for revenge". Peter's words would now haunt him for the rest of his life; for he understood the great wrong he had done her, when he forced her path to cross those of his fathers.

Everyone returned to the great hall to continue the celebration, but the mood had changed.  More somber and guarded, it never recovered. An hour after the dancing had begun the bride and groom made their way upstairs. The cheering continued until everyone realised that the newlyweds had closed the door to their separate bedrooms.

It bode not well that their brave little lady and their valiant Baron, began their wedded life, hiding from each other.

## Chapter 9

"Ye, misjudged the lady, my friend" Maximillian spoke to the hitherto silent Bruce.

"Lady? Ye dare call her a lady before me" Bruce bit back. "She rode outside the castle as a common woman would do, she spoke without respect and she challenged the Lord of Wilbert. No lady would do that!" he snarled.

"She stood beside her wedded lord, she stopped a son from fighting a father, and she defended an unjust charge against her. I see no wrong in that My Lord. I believe she is more of a lady than we acknowledge." Maximillian defended the woman he had instantly admired.

"A lady? Even my son does not know the name of her father. And Rosamund? There is no Emma of Rosamund. I am acquainted with the family of Rosamund and they have no daughter. And by the look on my son's face, I could see that he knew that too, even as he wed her, yet he chose to walk that path of destruction." Bruce snapped back

"Mayhaps he knows, this lady, is whom he needed in his life, My Lord." Maximillian added.

"I saw no quality worth admiring in her. Why do ye defend the maid?" Bruce gave vent to his anger with those words.

"Simply because, she reminded me of, the first Lady of Wilbert." Maximillian replied.

Bruce froze. After a moment he replied 'I understand not, how ye see a similarity, for they are as different as night from day. Raul's mother was rich, beautiful, demure and well versed. This one is none of the above."

"True my friend, she may show none of these qualities, but just like his mother, Raul's bride will do anything to protect yer son." came Maximillian's simple reply.

This did not go down well with Lord Bruce and he continued his journey in silence.

Bruce had been exhausted when he reached Kinsborough. They had ridden very hard, only stopping to change steeds and then keeping the same momentum going. They had covered the distance in half the time, only to arrive and find that Raul had already wed. That had been painful enough but to know that yer only son, wed without information or invitation was the part he found impossible to bear. His only son wed, without even letting his father know.

He knew the ultimatum had been a bad step from the moment it had been given, but he had never contemplated that his son would leave his father's home and within hours wed the first maid he saw. A maid who had no birth or breeding to speak off: No beauty or wealth to display. The only quality worth noting was her bold words and her fearless bearing but even that bordered on unruly insubordinate behavior.

His son should have done so much better. He would have to speak to Maja when she returned from her visit to her brother's home. They must be a way to correct this error. Maximillian was unwed and knew not what he spoke of. Nothing of the expectation a father has of his child.

"Bruce, it might have been wiser to halt the night at Kinsborough. We are all exhausted and could have well done with a hot meal and some rest".

"We can rest when we get to Wilbert. If ye wish to go back for a rest to Kinsborough, ye may ride back. I plan to continue on my journey." Bruce said stubbornly.

Maximillian looked up at the sky, as if to ask, how did I get myself into this. It was a waste of a question for he already knew the answer. When Bruce had sent the message to join him on the journey, he knew he had to come. Raul had been like a son to him ever since the time when he trained as his squire. They had been close, closer than Raul had ever been to his father. Whatever fondness the son once had for his father had ceased with the death of his mother.

When Maja had entered their home, ripping apart the family, it shattered the image Raul had had of a perfect father. On his mother's death, when he needed Bruce more than ever, Bruce had gone and married Maja. Lost and lonely, Raul had realised that the way to get his father's attention was to anger him. Unable to understand that the son was calling for his help, in desperation, Bruce had sent Raul to him.

It was the best thing that had happened for both Raul and him. Away from the home he associated with his mother,

Raul, proved himself an able squire and to Maximillian's immense pride, grew into a confident and courageous fighter. But then the Rosalie incident had happened. While Maximillian too did not believe Raul had truly loved Rosalie, he admitted that the situation had been badly handled by both Maja and Bruce.

And now years later, another mistake was going to take place and once again he was going to helplessly stand by and let his friend continue on an unwise path. Had he been just a friend he could have counseled Lord Bruce, but he was also his indebted knight. And an indebted knight did not counsel, he simply agreed.

Already Bruce had forced Raul to raise his sword. Raul, who had always been in control of himself! This night, he saw both father and son talk as enemies. It was not a good sign. For when it is made common knowledge that there is discord between family members, many vultures wait to scoop in.

He himself was happy with Raul's choice of a bride. Like Raul's mother, Emma had a quick wit but unlike Raul's mother she also had a quiet strength. A strength that if both Raul and Bruce were wise, they would keep mind of! When Bruce had referred to her as filth, he did not see anger on her face, he saw pity. It was the same look, Raul's mother had given Bruce, when he had first acknowledged his involvement with Maja. It had been in front of Maximillian. Lady Christina too had merely looked at her husband with that pitiful gaze and then taking her five year old son's hand had suggested that they go and look at the new piglets.

Lost in thought, he momentarily forgot where he was. When his mind returned him to the present almost a quarter into the hour later, Maximillian noted that Bruce held his heart while sweat covered his brow. Before he could grab hold of Bruce he saw him slide from his steed. His forehead was covered in huge droplets of sweat and his face crunched up in pain.

Maximillian knew the symptoms well. It was what happened before the heart weakened. He also knew that riding back to Wilbert was now, no longer a possibility. Sending word with one of his knights he requested for Raul to come with a cart, he laid Bruce on a pallet of leaves, wiped his brow with watered cloth and prayed for this danger to pass.

He looked back in the direction the knight had taken and already he was out of view. As long as the knight maintained that speed then help should be back before the night sky became any darker.

Chapter 10

The guards alerted all at Kinsborough that a rider approached their castle, armed but alone. Before the identity could be verified, Raul and Rowan had already reached the ward, dressed in chainmail and armed with their swords. It was almost as if they expected an attack during the night and had slept in their battle gear. Sir Peter picked up on Raul's silent communication and once again accepted his position as Emma's protector.

By the time Emma had dressed and come out of her room, Raul was at the gate, which was being raised after the guards had checked the identity of the rider and the rider had followed their command that he leave his weapon at the gate.

"My Lord" the rider addressed. "I am Sir Marcus of Dushire, once squire to yer father. I come at Sir Maximillian's command, to seek yer help. Lord Bruce suffered a fall as we rode away. It appears his heart has weakened for he fell to the ground holding his chest. Sir Maximillian urges ye rush to them with a cart. It does not appear that Lord Bruce will be able to continue on his journey in his condition."

"Is this a ruse or do ye tell me the truth? As a knight I ask on all ye hold sacred." Raul queried fearing that it could be a trap to force an annulment.

"I pledge it on all I hold sacred, My Lord" the knight replied. A knight's most valued asset was his chivalry and word. For a knight to breach the code of chivalry was akin to choosing dishonor. And no knight would allow himself to live with that.

Within moments of this pledge, Raul was seated on Daktonian, Rowan and twelve other knights were mounted on their steeds. A cart was prepared with a packhorse attached to it, so that the gentler pace would enable Raul to bring his father back with as little discomfort at possible.

Raul was just about to send a message to Emma, when she appeared from the cooking room. As she raced towards him unmindful that she had not secured her hair, Raul was forced to truly see it for the first time. It blew away from her face, gently pushed back by the breeze she created with her movement. She no longer applied the soot to her skin. It now shone in the night light. As he watched the vision of beauty run towards him, he yet again wondered how he had thought her plain.

"My Lord, I heard from Winifred. This is an infusion that will be helpful to him. Make yer father drink at least half of it. I understand the physician is away? I nursed my father, I know only a little but I can aid." Emma informed.

"Thank ye. I will ask Peter to aid ye in the arrangements here. Get the squires to help ye as well. I do not know what condition I will find my father in, but I believe if he is still alive, he will need care." Raul said, taking the container from her.

"Aye My Lord" Emma replied

"And My Lady, ye must remain in Sir Peter's view at all times until I return." he concluded.

"Do ye distrust yer father so?" she queried.

"I no longer know my father as I once did. It is best to be careful when ye have a man so displeased with his son." he replied.

"Then ye My Lord, must remain in Sir Rowan's view." she smiled with those words.

"I do not jest, My Lady Emma" he added with a grin.

"Nor I, My Lord, I am safe within yer castle; the trouble lies outside the castle and ye ride into it." she said.

"I may not trust my father at this moment, I do trust Sir Maximillian. I will return safely, of this I promise." Raul assured her, but noted that his assurance did not erase the creases from her brow.

"God speed then My Lord but pray heed the fact that Sir Maximillian was not able to stop yer father's words before, he may not be able to stop yer father's actions now." She warned.

Seeing Peter approaching him, he called "I leave my lady in yer care again Peter. My father returns with me. Ye both may look to the arrangements. And when we return, see that my father's men are disarmed when they enter the castle. Our hospitality must not be mistaken for weakness and an opportunity to attack." he cautioned.

"God speed Raul, go assured yer lady will be safe, as will remain, yer castle." Peter spoke as he reached Daktonian

Raul reached down and clasped the palm of his friend, then bowing to Emma he rode off. Sir Rowan waited at the gate and together they followed the messenger. Fifteen galloping steeds created a dust storm and when that settled, Raul was no longer in sight.

Once the drawbridge had been raised again and the gate lowered, Emma and Peter moved to the great hall.

"How sad, that a son so distrusts his father. Surely Lord Wilbert would not attack his own child?" Emma queried.

"My Lady, since his second marriage, Lord Wilbert, decides not for himself. A man not in control of his own mind is easily swayed and just as easily used. Hindsight is a wonderful thing, but it is a wasted gift, if it makes one wiser after sufferance. The baron prefers precaution." Sir Peter replied.

"And do ye believe his precaution is justified?" she asked further.

"He lived through a difficult childhood, a dangerous youth and a violent adulthood, yet he survived to wed. That was due to caution, My Lady. Many would still gain by his capture or death, my lord is well aware of that." he replied somberly.

"Surely ye do not include his father?" she questioned

"As I said earlier My Lady, a man, not in control of his own mind, is easily swayed and just as easily used. And a woman can achieve much when a man surrenders his mind to her control." he repeated

At that point, they reached the great hall and began to discuss the arrangements.

"I am sure my lord would like one of the rooms above be readied but I believe it best Lord Bruce stay in the great hall. A portion can be partitioned off by hanging these thick tapestries on wooden frames. Lord Bruce will then be near his knights for I believe he will object to our presence otherwise. The wash room and the latrine are also within easy walking distance. When he is better he will also want to use the bailey for his walks" Emma remarked.

"I saw ye give medicine for the Lord. It is not a common knowledge to have." Peter asked.

"My father too, suffered the same. It took him three moons before he was well enough to ride again. He asked for much care and much entertainment during that time." she smiled back.

"And did he get well?" Sir Peter questioned

"Of course Sir Peter, after all, it was I that cared for him." she gloated back.

"Well then My Lady, let us hope ye have the patience of a saint, for Lord Bruce, is one who demands much and faults all. Three moons will seem like purgatory." he smiled.

While they conversed, the carpenter hurried to make two frames by nailing wooden logs and placing them in hollowed stumps so that they remained upright. The squires pulled down the heavy tapestries and placed them over the frames. Sheeting from the bed upstairs was brought down and hung between them so as a make a door of cloth. Large lamps were placed inside to ensure there was enough light though the night.

Emma then placed a bowl of hot water with crushed mint leaves so that the air was infused with its smell. She knew it had helped her father breathe easier. She also asked the cook to prepare a thin broth for Lord Bruce and a thicker one for his knights. There was enough bread so it was simply warmed up and kept in readiness.

Just as Emma excused herself to go and ready herself in her room, the guards alerted the arrival of the riders. Time was not wasted in verifying their identity this time as the Baron was with the party, instead the draw bridge was lowered and the gate re-opened.

As they rode in, Emma could see Lord Bruce lying prone in the cart. Raul and Maximillian rode on either side. Rowan rode by Raul, an uncovered sword in his hand. It was sign enough for Emma that all was yet, not well between father and son.

Sir Peter had already rushed out to meet Raul. Emma watched from atop the steps as Lord Bruce's knights carefully carried him in. Raul and Peter spoke as they walked back. While still in conversation with Peter, Raul looked up to catch Emma's gaze. He bowed very slightly. In that look, Emma realized that for all his claim, he was deeply attached to his father, and truly worried about his condition. With her smile, she tried to assure him that he would have her support.

As they entered the great hall, Sir Peter directed the knights to the prepared area. There, they carefully placed Lord Bruce in the center of the bed and removed his stockings and leggings. His hauberk had already been removed to release the pressure off his chest.

Lord Bruce was awake but weakened by the attack. Worse he was clearly upset at having to be at Kinsborough and accepting the hospitality of his son.

"He would not take it. He accused me of trying to poison him." remarked Raul as he returned the jar to her.

"The physician has not returned. Two of yer knights are out looking for another physician who may be residing with yer neighbouring lords." She informed him.

"He faces death yet prefers no help from Kinsborough or me. He refused to even let me touch him." Raul continued in a normal tone, but his eyes revealed his pain.

"My Lord, men when they are ill, talk as a child. And when they are scared they lash out at those who are dear. Ye would not pay heed to the angry words of a babe. It would be just as wise not to pay heed to him until he is well." She replied.

"What if the physician does not come in time?" Raul worried aloud. He was a warrior and could help with broken bones and bleeding wounds, but the heart, he knew nothing about.

"My Lord, I have some experience with Lord Bruce's condition. He will not give me his permission to attend; I ask yers, so I may care for him until the physician arrives."

"Peter spoke of yer talk with him, but there lies a very great risk in what ye ask. If he does not get well, the blame will be placed at our door by his bride." Raul explained.

Emma thought a moment. How terrible that a child was scared to care for his parent, for fear of blame! After Lord Bruce's open dislike of Emma, her care would be under close scrutiny. But was that enough excuse for not helping a man that ailed? It took a few moments to decide but she came to the conclusion that nothing was worth inaction.

"Blame will be placed whether we help or not. It is better we are blamed for helping than be charged for not? I will go to yer father. He must have that infusion soon. The Mugworth, Hawthorne, Rosehip, and Comfrey will help."

"Was yer father, in the same condition?" he asked

"Worse My Lord, yer father still fights us, that is a good sign. Mine, was simply glad he was breathing and gave up all other fight." she replied.

With that she took the jar she held and walked to Lord Bruce's bedside.

"My Lord!" she whispered.

"Do not allow her near me." Lord Bruce replied with his eyes still closed.

"Ye ask that which is too late, I am already beside ye, My Lord." she replied gently.

"Then ask her to leave. I care not for her presence." he tried to growl but his heart had taken that strength away.

"My Lord, I bring two different tidings, which would ye like first, the good tiding or the bad one?" she said softly.

That got Lord Bruce's attention. He lifted one eyelid.

"Since ye are the bearer of the tiding, I see no difference in what ye will have to say." he barked but again the sound came out as a whimper.

"Ye judge incorrectly My Lord, I am the one that bears the good tiding, the physician if he get here in time, will bear the bad." she gave him a faint smile as she said the words.

"Well then I think I shall wait for the physician, for I prefer his bad news." he replied.

"Sir Maximillian, it is best ye now send for yer own physician from Wilbert. My Lord's physician is away from Kinsborough. And the two knights that were sent earlier to get a physician from the neighbouring lords have not returned and may not return for a while. I am the only one with a little knowledge for my father suffered the same as yer lord, but I have much to do with a castle full of visitors, so if yer lord does not need my help, I will go and help where I am truly needed."

With that she began to walk away, silently praying that Lord Bruce would stop her. He needed to drink the infusion soon. The weakened heart needed its curative qualities. If there was no change within an hour they would have to bleed him, for it is what the physician's do. Her father's physician had said that the blood sometimes creates little balls and if that is not bled out, it could stick within the heart or the head. The next two nights would be delicate. Even if he survived that, he would need weeks of rest.

Giving up hope, she looked at Raul standing at the exit. His smile, made her feel better but it did not take away the feeling that comes with failure.

"Stop the maid." she heard the words she was waiting for. Faint now, but still audible.

Ignoring him she continued to proceed out.

"Stop Raul's bride." he commanded again, but his voice seemed even weaker.

Emma ceased walking, slowly turned and walked back to him.

"Maximillian tell her, she must also drink what it is she gives me. I have heard many fathers-in- law being poisoned with even holy water by their daughters-in-law. And this one stands to gain much by my death. She will make herself Lady Wilbert." he uttered, though his voice was still low.

Raul who had been standing by the exit came forward and touched Emma's arm.

"Enough, ye may leave Emma. Some things do not alter where my father is concerned." he said, trying to pull Emma back.

Shrugging his arm she said to him, "It matters not what he says, it matters that he drinks this. Let me try. Please." she pleaded.

Raul removed his hand but remained by her side. As Emma moved closer, so did Raul.

"Sir Maximillian, there are some goblets by the bed, if I may have two of them." she requested.

She filled a quarter of one and three quarters of the other. Taking the goblet with the lesser amount she drained it in one gulf, dreading the taste for she knew it would be bitter. She was not wrong.

"It is yer turn next, My Lord." saying she motioned for Marcus, the knight by his side to lift Lord Bruce's head and gently touch the goblet to his lips tipping about a spoonful of the liquid and then quickly moving back herself.

As she expected, he spat it out with the words, "This is worse than poison. What do ye give me in this?" he asked.

'My Lord, it contains Hawthorne, Rosehip, Mugwort, Comfrey, and Nettle. Tomorrow if I can find it, I will add Parsley and Garlic to it. And it is best that ye develop a liking for it, for it will be yer friend for quite a while yet, My Lord." She answered calmly.

"Give Raul some first. He neither loves ye nor me. If we die, he will gain by both our deaths." Bruce argued.

By now Raul had had enough of his father's games. Grabbing the goblet from Emma's hand he drained it down in one gulp, threw the empty goblet on the bed, and walked out of the room.

"That man has no patience. Does he not know I am dying?" Lord Bruce worded.

"My Lord, I will make sure he is aware of it, before he next comes to see ye" Emma replied noting that Maximillian was trying hard to hold back his laughter.

"Now My Lord, will ye please have the infusion. Surely it is not that bad, for even a maid like me could stomach the bitter taste." Emma pleaded again, for Lord Bruce was wasting precious time.

"Maximillian, ye are to stand guard. If anything happens to me, tell the king, my son's bride forced me to have this vile drink." he grumbled.

This was authority enough. Emma quickly filled the goblet and between Maximillian and Marcus, they managed to get him to drink it all, in small sips accompanied by huge grunts and complaints. Once he had emptied the goblet,

Emma asked for several stools. Placing one near him, she sat down by his bed.

"I cannot sleep if she is going to gawk at me." came another complaint.

Without a word, Emma stood up, asked Maximillian to call her if the Lord's condition changed, handed the wet cloth in her hand to him, curtsied to the Lord and simply walked out. Her job for the moment was done.

Smiling, she decided it would be too harsh to warn the Lord that she would be back in an hour with more of that vile concoction.

Chapter 11

Hour upon hour, Emma gave him the drink, and hour upon hour his grumbling increased. Raul did not return to see his father, but he walked past often. And if he went out of the great hall, Rowan or Peter was assigned to remain within Emma's sight.

In the meanwhile Winifred organised the pallets for the knights and she also saw to it that they were given bread and broth before they lay down.

When the rooster crowed and daylight lit up the hall, Emma returned to give the Lord Wilbert his sixth goblet. Her heart hurt to see him struggle through the sips. She knew it was bitter to the tongue, and when ye lie helpless in a bed, commanded to drink the bitter liquid, it makes the task even more unpalatable.

"My Lord, I wish I could make this more bearable. But to work it must not be diluted nor mixed with anything that will take away its power to heal." Emma spoke softly as the last sip emptied the goblet.

For a second Lord Bruce looked at her almost with affection, but the words that came out next, showed no improvement, "If that be true, how is it that I do not see regret in yer eyes, I see joy?"

Emma once again smiled and then gently replied "My Lord, maybe they reflect what is in yers!"

Lord Bruce was so stunned by her response that he was unable to reply for some moments. When he was about to voice himself, Winifred arrived with the thin broth and the warm bread and Lord Bruce actually seemed disappointed that their conversation had come to an end. They all waited in an uncomfortable silence while the broth cooled.

A second Wilbert knight had taken the place of the first, and when the broth was cooler, he fed Lord Bruce while Emma remained seated by the bed. Lord Bruce could only manage half the bowl and a tiny portion of the bread roll, but it was a good sign that he was able to eat.

As the tray was being removed, Maximillian arrived with Kinsborough's own physician. Emma was never gladder to see anyone. The responsibility that she had placed on herself could now be transferred to the physician. Emma moved out while he checked on the Lord and returned to hear the positive diagnosis. While the Lord would need many days of rest and would not be able to return to Wilbert for at least a week, he was doing well and would not require any bleeding. He inquired about the contents of the infusion and was astonished that the Lady of Kinsbourough was so well informed. She had won the respect of one more man at Kinsborough but had raised more questions about her true identity.

Leaving Lord Wilbert in the care of the physician, Emma departed for her room. Outside, Raul stood in conversation with Peter. Rowan had been asked to rest, so that he would be in charge when Peter and Raul took their sleep.

As Emma came through the makeshift screen, Raul and Peter ceased their conversation. Raul looked at his bride of not yet a day, noted her exhaustion and at once left Peter's side to walk to hers.

"I dared not take ye from my father's side earlier but now that the physician is here, I want ye to go straight to bed. I will command that ye are not disturbed." he spoke with concern.

"I will My Lord, for I fear, the night is taking its toll. I see ye both are in no better condition." She remarked.

"Unlike ye, we have rested on the pallets down here" he replied.

"But not slept My Lord. As yer father gets better, he will need ye more. It is best ye too, rest now." she added.

"I am well" he replied.

"But My Lord, in yer eyes I see weariness." she said.

"Maybe My Lady, they reflect what is in yers." Raul softly added.

Emma knew then that he had overheard her conversation with his father. She wanted to say something clever back, but she was much too tired to bring wit into her conversation now. From the time she had been captured, to this moment as she stood before her wedded lord, she had not had a wink of sleep. As she looked at Raul, all she could think of was getting to her room and at the thought of sleep, her eyelids drooped shut.

Raul reached out his arm to steady her and held her firmly at the elbows. Then throwing protocol to the winds, he lifted her and carried her up to the stairwell. His grip tightening as she tried to push away and lower herself to the floor.

"My Lord" she called and was ignored by Raul.

'MY LORD" she called again, clearly anxious this time.

"What is it My Lady?" he questioned, feigning irritation.

"I hope ye have done this before for if ye drop me, it is a long way for me to fall." she asked with dismay.

Raul's laughter rang out in the great hall and the stairwell as Emma clung to his garment. The stairwell had no railing. If Raul missed his footing, there really would be nothing to prevent their fall - a fact that seemed not to worry her husband.

As they reached the landing, an astonished guard scrambled to move out of their way. As he approached her room, Ralph stopped and waited until the guard had opened the door. Walking in, he lowered her onto the bed

"Winifred" he called.

"Aye My Lord" Winifred rushed in to Emma's room.

"See that yer lady sleeps and stay with her until she wakes. The guards will remain here but we have many who are not of Kinsborough so keep the door bolted from inside." he ordered.

"Aye My Lord."

"Emma I…." Raul turned and then stopped. Smiling, he looked at his sleeping bride who was totally dead to the world.

"Yer bride did well this day, My Lord." Winifred spoke.

"Too well Winifred. Much too well, for a kitchen maid." his comment, brought a frown to Winifred's brow.

"Do ye doubt her claim?" Winifred asked.

"The claim was never made by her. It was made for her." he replied.

"But did she affirm the claim?" Winifred continued.

"Nay, but neither did she refute it." he added.

"My Lord, who, do ye believe my lady is then?" Winifred queried.

"According to Sir Maximillian, my father knows the house of Rosamund and they are not of much consequence and cannot claim the title of lord. They do not have a daughter" he answered.

"That would be right My Lord, for my lady said her father was the steward there not the lord." Winifred clarified.

"The steward at Rosamund, is newly married, and has but one child, a son of only six" Raul clarified further.

"Who then is my lady and why My Lord is she hiding her identity?" Winifred questioned .

"The answer lies within her." He replied.

"Why not ask my lady, for the truth of it?" Winifred added.

"Nay, she must never find out that we know that she is not Emma of Rosamund. It would likely make her bolt again. Once my father has left, I will work on solving this riddle but until then only Peter, Rowan, Sir Maximillian, ye and I know, my bride is not who she claims to be." Raul added.

"If ye father knows she is not from Rosamund then he too will be aware of the truth." Winifred expressed her concern

"My father only knows that she is not the Lady of Rosamund." he explained.

"That is fine then My Lord, for she had never called herself a lady." Winifred cleared.

"That is the very issue of it Winifred. She is a lady, but from where?" he asked.

"Why believe that My Lord?" she queried.

"No one, but a lady, would have dared jest with the Lord of Wilbert." he replied.

"My Lord I can converse with my lady and see if she tells of her past." Winifred offered.

"Nay, for ye rightly said, my bride is a flighty one. I cannot risk her trying to escape again" Raul said, then looking at his bride one more time exited the room.

Chapter 12

When Emma woke, the sky was dark again. The movement in the room alerted her to Winifred's presence.

"How long have I been abed Winifred?" she asked.

"Ye missed the hours between sunrise and sunset My Lady" Winifred illuminated.

"Heaven forbid, ye should have woken me before this. How fares Lord Wilbert?" she asked.

"He does well My Lady. The physician says there is much improvement." Winifred enlightened.

"I am glad to hear ye, and, my lord, is he rested too?" Emma queried.

"He is in the great hall. Both father and son have asked after ye. I was to inform My Lord as soon as ye awoke." Winifred said.

"Later, for first Winifred, I need to have a bath. I smell worse than I did when the tallow was on me. The smell of that infusion is truly unbearable." Emma smiled.

"My Lady the bath below is being used, but my lord's bath is free. My Lord is below in the great hall. He will not come up now so ye may bath there." Winifred offered.

"Then I must hasten and have it." added Emma.

Winifred ordered warm water to be brought up in pails while she took Emma over to Raul's room. In a little alcove off his bedroom rested a wooden contraption.

"Come see My Lady. It is a very clever creation by the Baron. Ye fill the water from the top. Once the bath is over, ye remove the wooded blocks and the barrel tilts and lets all the water out. That hole in the wall is attached to a pipe that drains the water outside the castle wall. The bath ye used below works in the same way My Lady except that we use that water to wash the pavements."

'This is indeed clever." Emma liked the idea very much. If wood was not a scarce commodity, she would have baths made for everyone.

And some fifteen minutes later, Emma had completed her bath, and was feeling refreshed again.

Dressed in one of her own pale blue garment, she walked out of the room. In one hand she held the pail with her washed clothes; with the other she dried her hair with a cotton sheet. Hearing footsteps she called to Winifred to take the pail so that she could hang them to dry below. Not expecting Raul, his entrance left her speechless.

Surprised to see his bride coming from his room, he glanced around for Winifred.

"She went to get me supper since all have already eaten below. I needed a bath and Winifred thought this one would be best. We did not think ye would return so soon. How is yer father, My Lord?" she blurted trying to overcome the awkwardness of being caught in his room.

"He does well and is much improved. His anger seems to have returned to the physician's dismay. But between his knights, they keep him bound to his bed." Raul said smiling.

"If he is willing, I will visit him once I am dressed." she added.

"He rests now but if ye wish to see him, I will take ye after ye have eaten. He asked for ye several times." he replied.

"In polite terms I hope?" she asked with her impish grin.

"Let me see, his exact words were 'Where is that lady who tortures me with her vile concoctions? She leaves me to suffer alone while she partakes of tasty morsels." Raul replied.

"Ah he is feeling better, for he remembers he is Lord Wilbert again." Emma laughed.

Raul looked at his bride. Just yesterday she stood terrified betwixt a jeering crowd bidding on her as though she was an animal. Today she stood in front of him, as his wedded bride, fearless and secure and not afraid of communication.  He tried to recall the moment when that change occurred. She was still fearful as she tried to escape. And then he worked out the exact moment when she changed from the meek Emma to the brave one that now stood in front of him. It was the moment he promised her that he would make no demands. Raul was no longer sure if this knowledge was good for his ego.

He knew she was a lady in hiding. He knew she feared demands and expectations. Was it possible that she had once been betrothed to a cruel man or been widowed by a demanding lord? It was certain she was running from something or someone. The question remained, why and who?

"I say that in jest My Lord, it is not to insult yer father." he heard Emma's voice.

He looked puzzled at her comment.

"Ye remained quiet My Lord" she added

"Pardon, I was lost in thought. Come I will carry yer pail back to yer room." Raul offered.

Handing over the pail she turned to tie back her hair.

"Ye hide it well, yet it should fly free as now, without grease or soot." Raul remarked.

"Winifred has spoken to ye of it?" Emma queried.

"Nay, Winifred would not speak of such personal matters. When I carried ye up, the grease and the soot stained my garment." he replied

"Pardon My Lord, if ye hand me that garment I will wash it off" she offered.

"It was washed off this morn. Why do ye ruin such beautiful hair with grease?" he asked.

"It promotes growth My Lord. I would have hair that goes to my knee." she replied.

"Then do not cut it." he replied

Emma stared at Raul for a moment then laughing said, "That would be practical like a man, My Lord, but not challenging like a maid."

Raul had begun to enjoy her banters. She was clever, with wit and knowledge. And within just hours he found himself, looking forward to their conversations. He offered to sit with her while she ate, and graciously waited at the landing while she completed her dressing.

When Winifred appeared with a tray, and Emma opened the door, Raul was pleased to see that Emma had left her hair in a loose plait. There was not a trace of grease or soot. Yet again he wondered how he had first thought her plain. It was a question that would arise time and again in the next few months.

Refusing to share her meal, he did accept a glass of warm mead. As she ate, they talked of Kinsborough and his grandfather. The memories were joyous ones that spoke of a loving relationship and a strong bond. Then they spoke of his mother and Emma knew at once, why Raul chose to distance himself from his father. He could not forget the betrayal by his father, and the pain and humiliation Lady Christina had endured as a result of it. And since it was too late to correct either of those wrongs, he had found a way to remain loyal to his mother, by keeping his father at a distance.

Raul refused to speak of Maja except to say, "God protected us from the birth of a demon in our family but then gave my father the privilege of importing one in with his second marriage"

There was much more she wanted to ask him, of his time as a squire, of his battles and wars. And of his hopes and dreams for Kinsborough. But as soon as her supper was over, Lord Bruce asked for his son and the couple left together to visit him.

As soon as the curtain was lifted to let her through, she heard Lord Bruce's voice rise to challenge her patience again.

"Did she ask ye to make this drink more bitter? For I am sure, it tastes viler with each goblet." he roared at the physician. But she was glad that at least his voice was clear and strong. It was almost as strong as when he had first uttered the word to his son "So ye are wed?"

Emma waited until the physician had completed his task and the goblet was empty before she came forward.

"My Lord, ye look better" with that she curtsied.

'She says that so she can take the credit. Tell her that she did not attend to me this whole day and therefore the credit belongs to ye, not her." he addressed the physician who looked apologetically at Emma.

"I would not dare take credit, when yer temper is still so foul My Lord. Had my concoction worked, My Lord's tongue would have been sweetened as well." Emma remarked, daring Lord Bruce to admonish her for her audacity.

"Yer rest has apparently not sweetened yers either." he retorted.

"Touche! My Lord" she curtsied again. Raul looked at Emma as soon as she had uttered the expression. A Norman word, how does she learn of that? He thought.

Raul's heritage was a Norman one, and while several generations had made him more English than Norman, the family still kept aspects of the Norman culture alive. The language was one, and her word belonged to it. It spoke of a Norman heritage for her and gave him his first clue.

Emma too realised her error. Her mother was Norman and had taught both her children some of the Norman ways. And while Emma was proud of her dual heritage, revealing her Norman link would make it easy for her to be traced, for there were not many Norman brides in England when her mother had wed her father. She had noted Raul's head jerk at her expression. She would have to be careful in future.

"Well are ye going to stand there or will ye sit and converse with me?" Lord Bruce asked suddenly,

"If the Lord of Kinsborough permits me, I am happy to sit with ye My Lord." she replied and looked at Raul, seeking his permission.

Emma wished to make it clear to all especially Lord Bruce, that while she would do his bidding, her loyalty would always be to Baron Raul. It was her Lord's name that was going to give her protection and it was important to give its strength the honour is deserved.

If Lord Bruce was surprised by her words, Raul was more so. How could she have guessed the game his father was playing and dealt with it so superbly? Raul knew that Emma and he shared no affection, yet her words, filled him with pride, and with one other emotion. Gratitude! With her words she had stamped her allegiance, to him and to Kinsborough. And he knew, both were now in her safe hands.

"My Lady is free to converse. I have matters to attend, and then I shall be back to walk ye to yer room." with that he bowed to his father and left.

Emma sat with her father-in-law for the next quarter hour. For the first half he seemed amiable though he expressed his desire to return to Wilbert several times. And each time, Emma assured him that as soon as the physician permitted Lord Bruce to travel; his son would ensure that his journey back was made comfortable.

And then suddenly he brought about the topic of Rosamund.

"My son said ye were from Rosamund?" he queried.

'Nay My Lord, my father was steward there." she replied.

"And where is yer father." she queried further.

"He has passed on My Lord." she replied.

"And his name?" he interrogated.

"Peter, steward of Rosemund, My Lord," she replied.

"Ye lie, for I am acquainted with the house of Rosamund and I have never met a Peter there." he bluffed

"It is not surprising, for the lords that visited Rosemund seldom acquainted themselves with those in service there." She replied in an even voice that did not display the nerves she felt inside. She also did not correct him when he referred to Rosemund as Rosamund. The more things remained confused the better it was for her.

Lord Wilbert was silent a moment. She was right, when Lords visited each other they seldom if ever met with the domestic staff. He himself did not even know the names of those his bride and he employed. But as soon as he was well enough to travel he would pay the house of Rosamund a visit. There was much he wanted to find out about his son's bride.

When Raul came to collect Emma he noted that she was glad of his arrival and even gladder to leave his father's bedside and wondered at what had occurred. That she was not comfortable convinced him that he would have to ensure that she was not left alone again. He had learnt to handle his father's insults and shielded himself against his father's abuse, but his bride, had not had time to learn the best way to handle his father.

"Ye will come on the morrow?" Lord Wilbert asked of Emma as she was leaving.

"Aye My Lord, I will come with yer son, so as not to tire ye with too many visits. It is best ye rest and converse little."

she replied. Raul reassessed his thought. He did not have to worry about Emma and his father anymore. She was capable of dealing with him.

Suddenly Lord Wilbert laughed, "Yer bride is a clever one, Raul. I see now, how she ensnared ye into marriage." It sounded as if he was jesting.

"My Lord has been misinformed; I am innocent of this charge. If yer son stands wedded today My Lord, it is with yer blessing. That he is wedded to me, is also of yer doing." Emma cut in with a smile

Again Lord Wilbert laughed before saying "Ye are mistaken, for had it been my doing, my son would have wed a lady."

Before Emma could respond, Raul spoke up,

"Ye are both ill-informed, I wed as I was fated and the Baron of Kinsborough has wed his Lady."

With his comment, what had been a clever jest between his father and bride came to an end. He did not mind the jest, but their conversation was bordering on accusations. It would not do for either to follow that path. And he wanted all to know, that no matter what their personal understanding, Emma was now Lady of Kinsborough and more importantly she was his bride and therefore under his protection.

Emma was partly right that his father was instrumental in his marriage but he had not married to obey his father's wishes. He had married to impede his father's desires.

When the silence that followed became awkward, he suggested they leave.

"Father we leave ye to rest. I will bring my lady after she has broken fast in the morn. If ye need him, the physician rest outside yer room. Get word sent to me if ye need me to come." With that he bowed and directed Emma to lead.

She curtsied to Lord Wilbert and left as directed.

As soon as they left the great hall, Raul offered to walk with Emma on the wall walk. He often did that before going to bed. He did his thinking if he walked alone. And he did his planning if he walked with Rowan or Peter. Tonight he wished to have Emma's company, and was glad when she accepted.

"My father has no delicacy of language. I offer ye the same advice, ye gave me earlier. He is angry and his words are best ignored." Raul said as they stepped onto the wall walk

"His words do not concern me, My Lord, for it is not I that anger him, it is yer bride."

she replied.

"My bride and ye, are one and the same now." he answered.

"True My Lord, but he does not dislike me until he remembers who I have wed." she replied, with the words that led to Raul's next query.

"What did he say that made ye think so?" he questioned.

"He asks for my company yet disapproves of my position here." she replied

"He would have disapproved of anyone who was in yer place. His disappointment is not in ye, but in me." he replied.

"My Lord, I do not believe he is disappointed in ye, he just fears he sees a better man than himself. It is a knowledge not welcomed by most fathers." she replied.

The words which were mere observation for Emma, were infused with deeper meaning for Raul. No woman in his entire life had paid him the tribute his bride just had, not even Rosalie. And he had thought that Rosalie had loved him.

"Ah so now ye study the human mind as well" he remarked instead.

"Nay My Lord, that I have mastered." she replied with a smile.

"If that be so, then pray tell me, how do we change this situation between my father and me?" he asked.

"Let not yer love for your mother, colour yer thoughts of yer father. He knows he has erred and that it cannot be undone. Let that be enough." she replied.

"What observation makes My Lady say that?" he queried.

"My Lord, had ye been on what ye thought was yer deathbed, would ye not have wanted the woman ye married for love, by yer side. I know if I were dying, and my beloved lord was afar, it would kill me before the ailment did. Yet Lord Wilbert asks his lady to remain at Wilbert. Surely Sir Maximillian could have cared for his holding at Wilbert and his lady could have been by his side." she concluded.

"My father has little value for such emotions. He prides himself in being practical. It was practical to have a mistress while he was wed to my mother. It was practical to send me away after my mother's death. And it is practical for him to have me near him now." he replied.

"How is what he does, any different My Lord, from what we do? Are we not wed because it was practical for us to wed each other?" she alleged.

"We wed, not to be practical, but because it was necessary." he tried to argue the point.

"Change the name if ye will, it will matter not, for where the heart is not involved, there the word 'practical' applies." she clarified.

"Ye tell me I am better than my father, yet ye equal my actions to his?" he asked in confusion.

"My Lord, when I praised ye earlier, it was yer judgment I spoke well off. Do ye not agree that of the two, ye have chosen the better bride?" With that she broke into a gentle laugh and that laughter rang through the silent night.

Her words brought Raul to a halt and her laughter, brought a smile to his lips. She had bested him again! His lady, of God only knew where!

When Emma realised that Raul no longer walked beside her, she stopped and turned to check. What she saw was not her lord friend, but a man standing and staring at her, a soft smile playing on his lips, and his eyes glittering with admiration.

"I best get some rest now, My Lord." saying she retreated her steps and went to walk past him

"Emma!" he stopped her with her name, "I will not dishonor my word."

Emma looked at him for several moments in silence. He had understood her fear, her need to retreat. And he promised again, to honour her wishes.

"Then My Lord, I shall look forward to our walk this time tomorrow." with that she walked towards the stairwell, leaving Raul, no option but to follow.

Escorting her to her room, Raul bid her good night and returned back to the great hall in search of Rowan. Her laughter still rang in his ear, and her mirth filled eyes mocked his sanity.

While his father was at Kinsborough he had assigned the task of training his knights to Rowan.  Now he wanted to discuss their progress and went in search of him for he knew sleep would not come for many an hour.

Chapter 13

Nearly a week passed in which they followed the same routine. After breaking fast she would visit with Lord Wilbert, growing more confident of her position with each day that went and conversing longer with each visit. After that morning duty, she busied herself overseeing the care of the knights.

During the afternoon, with the physician she visited the families that lived in Kinsborough. He had decided that the lady had more than adequate knowledge to diagnose treatment as well and enjoyed the opportunity to having someone of like mind to discuss his plants, herbs and treatments with.

Emma too loved this part of the day. She finally felt useful. It was her love for healing that led her onto the path of knowledge. She had learnt from all who had been willing to teach. Little bits of knowledge that compounded into a storehouse of information! Now as she debated the merits of various treatments, she decided that if the physician and she were to be able to truly help the people of Kinsborough and their neighbours, they needed to have the herbs available to them at all times.

A week after Lord Wilbert had arrived; a large piece of land had been marked off for the herb and vegetable garden. Between the physician and her, they carefully transplanted hundreds of plants from the surrounding areas into the castle. Raul ensured that she was adequately protected before he let them go on their venture outside the castle. Oft times, he followed at a distance, ensuring that his bride was safe.

He realised that his bride had a much greater plan in mind, when two days after she had claimed a part of his land as a vegetable and herb garden, she asked him as they strolled the wall-walk.

"My Lord, would we be able to build a large hall beside the garden"

"Let me guess My Lady, ye love yer plants so much that ye plan to move near them!" he teased.

"That thought had not crossed my mind, My Lord, but it does have merit." she bantered back

"Since that is an approval I cannot give, what is the real reason for the hall?" he queried.

"A sick room My Lord." she replied.

"Did I hear ye correctly My Lady, a sick room?" he quizzed.

"Aye, My Lord! It will be where the physician and I will treat the ill. Away from everyone else, it will be close to the herbs and if we have room available, people from yer neighbouring lords can also come here to be healed" she replied.

"And what inspired ye with this thought?" he asked.

"Yer father's stay My Lord, and the fear of not being able to treat him while the physician was away. If we have a sick room and two physicians at all times here, we will be able to look after and offer healing to anyone who needs help" she replied

"If ye open the gates to all, ye will weaken our stronghold. I cannot permit that." he replied.

"How does that weaken Kinsborough?" she questioned not understanding his defensive stand.

"Do ye recall when my father arrived I asked Peter to disarm all his knights. Even now only half of my knights sleep at any one time. The other half stay awake to watch over his. If ye open the gates of Kinsborough to all, the lives of my men will be as risk. The chance for an enemy entering our hold will greatly increase. Most lords also travel with armed knights. If ye offer healing to one, the rest will stay till the healing is done. For now we sleep in peace once the gates are secured. With strangers amidst us, that will not be so." he explained.

"And if we build the great hall outside the castle?" she queried

"Safety will remain the issue there too, My Lady, both of the physician that treats and the ill that come to be healed." he replied.

"My Lord it is a waste to have this knowledge yet not be able to use it to help others." her voice sounded defeated.

"I will build the great hall, but it will be within the castle and for its people only. Would that be acceptable?" he offered.

Raul knew Emma's plan was a good one. He himself had been treated by the Hospitallers. It was their initial care that paved the way to recovery. If her venture fared well, he would consider setting up a larger place secured by a second wall. But for the moment he was not going to offer more than what was practical.

To Emma, Raul's offer was like having a dream come to fruition. She would finally be able to do something of worth. Caring for the ill and the hurt! Caring for someone so that his last moments would not be alone lying wounded in a battlefield! She truly felt grateful, and so could not comprehend her next words.

"Ye offer half a mug of water, and ye ask if that will quench my thirst. It is not enough but ye give us a good start.  For that I am thankful." She conceded gratefully.

"I offer ye only half a mug? What My Lady do ye wish to ask of me, a whole pail?" he teased.

"Nay My Lord, I am not that greedy, I ask only for a full mug." she joshed back.

"I must beware yer requests in future My Lady, lest ye ask for the whole castle next." he added.

"My Lord, if I asked for this castle for a sick room it would only be right, for ye plan on joining the crusade anyway. Ye plan on leaving this large empty castle, to my care. To what purpose should I tend to its care? So that when ye are gone, another can fight and claim it as his own. If Kinsborough is made into a shelter for the injured and the sick, who like ye will be travelling far from their home, it would only be for the good. And our sire would offer his protection to this castle so that no one would dare attempt to attack it while ye are gone." she spoke.

While the thought was noble and selfless, the image of strangers walking through Kinsborough and of his bride spending her time with them instead of being with him was oddly depressing. Kinsborough had the right to have a happy lord and lady, a room full of boisterous and bold children, and a future that offered security and prosperity to its inhabitants. Instead his path was leaving Kinsborough without his protection, his lady without her lord, and the possibility of another grabbing Kinsborough and its lady from him.

The thought made him still. Had he not once said that Kinsborough would find its own lord again? Had he not been angered by his father's wish that his son forget his desire to become a Templar knight?

And yet the future that had seemed so right for him just days before, now no longer appeared as appealing. The thought of him, fighting another's battle while his bride stood alone and fought his, to save his castle, lifted bile to his throat.

A future that had not bothered him before now suffocated him and he realized that he no longer wanted that future. His present was what he wanted to cling on to, for only his present included Emma.

Peter had been right when he had warned Raul, that he had not taken the heart into consideration when he had first set out with his plan. But where Peter had been wrong was that it was not Emma's heart that needed watching, it was his.

"My Lord?" Emma questioned his silence

"Tell me My Lady, if I remained at Kinsborough, would ye give up this plan?" he asked.

Emma remained silent a while. She knew in her heart that she did not want him to leave, but she would not ask him to stay while he felt as if he was being held at ransom.

"My Lord, if ye stay now, ye would have wed me for naught. I believe I am right when I say that vexing yer father was not the only reason ye wed, My Lord, yer dream was the other reason. Ye longed to join the crusades and I was chosen so I would not stand in yer way.  Fear not, that I will alter yer castle. It shall remain as it is now and the sick room will only be for yer people." she replied.

Her reply was not well received by Raul's heart. This time his strategy had failed completely and it was too late to plan differently. Their ships had already sailed in different directions.

Chapter 14

Eight days after his arrival, Lord Bruce had gained enough strength to go for short walks around the bailey. This he did with Raul and Maximillian or with his own knights.

Every evening he played Chess with Emma who unlike most ladies, refused to let him win. While he admired that quality in Raul's bride, he took the opportunity of pointing out to her how unladylike such behavior was at every chance.

Emma noticed that Raul too was more patient with his father. What they shared could still not be called love, but a silent compromise had taken place betwixt them. Lord Bruce understood that Raul was now his own man, and he himself had started that process when he sent his son away as squire to Maximillian. And Raul realised that for all his bravado, his father truly needed him. He showed it in little acts such as refusing to sleep until Raul had bid him goodnight. It was Maximillian who noticed it first, and was glad of it.

On the morning of the ninth day, Lord Bruce received a missive from his bride, to say that unless he was actually dying, he needed to return to Wilbert for his knights and those of his neighbouring land had been involved in a skirmish. The news visibly upset Lord Bruce, and even the physician agreed that it would be best that Lord Bruce return home least he fret himself into illness again.

As Emma and Raul walked on the rampart that evening he began their conversation.

"My Lady, with my father as vulnerable as he is, I would travel with him to Wilbert and he plans on leaving in the morn." he said.

"I did feel it would be so. How long do ye plan yer stay there?" she replied.

"With father travelling in a cart, it will take longer to reach. I will stay but a day or two more and ensure his borders are safe. Whatever our faults and difference, he is my father and I would not permit, others to use our rift for their gain." he replied.

"I wonder at ye wanting to join the crusade, when ye so easily find yerself in the midst of battles, right here." she replied, her impish smile telling him she jested again.

"Battles?" he queried.

"Aye  My Lord, ye saved me from those men, ye rode not knowing if ye and yer father would battle, and now ye ride again, armed with yer sword." she replied.

"Those, My Lady, are not battles. Those are skirmishes and I do not ride to them, they beckon me." he answered.

"Precisely My Lord." she said looking him in the eye.

"Ye would have me not go?" he asked.

"Nay My Lord, I would have ye ask me to ride as well." she replied.

"Nay My Lady, ye are safer in Kinsborough. I will leave Sir Rowan and Sir Peter to guard ye."

"And who will watch yer back, My Lord?" she asked.

"I have other knights." he replied.

'If ye go My Lord, ye take Sir Peter or Sir Rowan with ye or I travel as well."

she declared.

"If that be yer options then I take Rowan with me." he replied.

"Ye leave a tedious task to Sir Peter, when ye leave him with my care" she remarked.

"It was he who assigned himself to be yer protector before we wed." Raul explained.

"How so My Lord?" she queried.

"Had ye not willingly walked to the altar, he would not have allowed me to wed ye" he explained. It was information that she cherished. Yet again she felt cared for.

The next morn, the party prepared to leave. At Maximillian and Raul's insistence, Lord Bruce agreed to travel in the cart.

As Emma came forward to bid him farewell, Lord Bruce looked at her for several moments, and then whispered "I still do not wish ye as my son's bride, but I would that ye had been my daughter". It was the closest he had ever got to giving her a compliment, but it was enough to make her cry.

After composing herself, she smiled and jested "My Lord, I still would not wish ye for a father" then added seriously ", but I am glad ye are my lord's sire"

As the cart left, Lord Bruce, turned and bid farewell.

Emma stood beside Winifred and returned the wave. She noted Raul lag to the back of the party. Then he turned and came to her.

"Take care of yerself Lady Emma. I will see ye soon"

God speed My Lord." she replied.

"Winifred…"he started.

"Aye My Lord, I know what ye will say. I will take care of yer lady." she promised.

With one last glance at Emma, he left.

That night was the longest Emma had ever spent. Winifred slept in her room and noted that her mistress remained restless. It was a good sign. The indifference was not a good thing. Sometimes marriage needs a reminder that two people dwell in it, not one.

When the sun rose, Emma did too. She made herself busy with her routine tasks. But everywhere she went, Raul had stamped his presence.

She kept herself busy, not even taking an afternoon rest as she normally did. By supper time, she was exhausted but made a determined effort to act normal. It did not work, for even the people of Kinsborough were missing their lord and their men and their gloom added to hers.

It seemed supper time became a norm for unannounced visitors. On Raul's first day away to his father's home, Maja arrived with her small retinue of two knights and one maid. The fact that neither Peter nor Winifred was happy about it, was no secret and their displeasure was openly shown on their faces. The fact that Maja lied about why she came, placed everyone on edge; as Lord Bruce had returned with his son, Maja had decided to come and see Emma for she felt while Raul was with his father he would be well looked after and she would not feel guilty about coming to see Emma. Adding that Lord Bruce had spoken so highly of Emma and the care she had given him, that Maja felt obligated to come and thank her personally.

"Lady Wilbert, ye are most welcome but I would have been more than willing to travel to Wilbert had ye sent a missive instead of taking the trouble to come yerself. I know how much ye must worry about Lord Bruce. I hope the journey did not tire him too much." Emma remarked.

"My Lord is well and endured the journey well enough. So ye are the lady, who so captivated Raul that he did not even wait to have his father attend his wedding"

Maja's choice of words did not sit well with Peter.

"I can only beg pardon on behalf of my lord and me, but we are glad that we had the good fortune of having both Lord Wilbert and ye, visit us so soon after." Emma replied.

"Well, at least ye have the grace to welcome me here, Raul has never invited me to Kinsborough." Maja's words were all that Peter needed to hear for it proved that Maja came without Raul's consent. He tried to catch Emma's eyes to say, 'do not permit her to stay' but Emma was lost in her own thoughts.

At Maja's words, Emma realised that she now faced a dilemma that must be solved with delicacy for she knew that Raul did not want Maja in his mother's home. That was why she had never been invited here. And her loyalty to Raul would not allow her to give Maja the chance to contaminate his mother's memory.

"Lady Wilbert, if my lord, has not invited ye earlier it must be because the rooms above stairs are currently in a state of repair. And with accommodation only available in the sick room, it would have made yer stay here uncomfortable." Emma found the excuse she wanted.

"I see, so where do ye sleep if the rooms above cannot be used" Maja asked suspecting falsehood.

"Most of us women, sleep in the sick room too Lady Wilbert" she replied.

"What is this sick room?" she asked.

"It is where we care for the ill and those who need healing. It is only partly constructed and lacks comfort" Emma replied.

"Well I will need to stay the night for it is too late to return to Wilbert. If ye can sleep in the sick room so can

I." Maja was adamant to remain at Wilbert until her work was done. She wanted Emma out of this marriage, either physically or at least emotionally.

"I will take ye there then, Lady Wilbert." Emma hastened, then having second thoughts, turning addressed Winifred.

"Winifred, take Lady Wilbert to the sick room. I will follow shortly for I have to make arrangements for the knights."

"Aye My Lady" with that Winifred led Maja out of the ward. When they had left, Emma turned to Peter.

"Sir Peter, pray organise the sleeping arrangements for Lady Wilbert's knights near Sir Rowan's knights for there is space there."

"Aye My Lady." Peter replied.

"And disarm them. I think that is the way, yer lord, says it." she whispered with a smile.

"The Baron would be very proud of ye had he been here to witness yer quick thinking My Lady" he said in hushed tones.

"I will believe as ye say for it gladdens my heart to hear it, but my lord is just as likely to be upset that I keep Lady Wilbert in the sick room." she replied.

"If he is upset at all, it will be, that Lady Wilbert stays or that ye place yerself in the sick room too My Lady. Not only is Winifred going to remain with ye, but so are Mary, Jane and two of the kitchen maids. They are to take turns to stay awake through the night. I know why ye chose the sick room, My Lady, but it is not secure." Peter warned.

"I understand yer concern, but while the sick room is not as safe, it is the only option I have. I do not believe my lord would permit, Lady Wilbert in his mother's room or his grand-father's"

"The second level where the women sleep could have done." he remarked.

"Nay Sir Peter, the keep is sacred to my lord, all of it." she replied.

"My Lady, Lady Wilbert is not to be trusted at all." Peter warned.

"I will keep note of yer words. For tonight, can ye ensure that the rooms upstairs are bolted and guards placed so no one goes above."

"Aye My Lady. And I will also post knights outside yer sick room who will keep vigil as well." he added.

"Thank ye, Sir Peter. Only one other person worried about me, as my lord and ye" she said.

When she saw Peter frown she added "My brother, though younger than me, he fret so about my safety."

"Is ye brother not alive then, My Lady?" he asked.

"Nay, Sir Peter, I lost him to the King and his endless battles." With tears threatening to fall, she turned and left in the direction of the kitchen.

Peter watched the empty space where his lady had stood. For a man to fight for the king he would have to be a knight and that would make his lady, a knight's sister. He would have to pass the clue on to Raul. But what worried him now was the bitterness and sadness that had infiltrated into his lady's voice. How would she feel, when she finds out that Raul too fights for the king?

Emma left instructions to send refreshments to the sick room and then went over herself.

There were already several pallets ready with sheets. Maja was seated on one when Emma entered the room. There was only one person in the sick room that night - a fact that Emma was grateful for.

Soon after Emma settled down, their refreshment arrived. Emma had already eaten supper but took a small helping to accompany Maja. With so many cases of poisoning, a guest rarely ate if the host did not.

An hour into their conversation, Emma realised that she may have erred in her decision to stay in the same place as Lady Wilbert, for Maja had spent a major portion of their conversation, inquiring about Emma's past. But worse was yet to come, for her next topic of conversation was Rosalie, the beautiful maiden who Raul had so loved that he had chosen to go to battle in the hope of dying, at her loss. That even now upon entering Wilbert, Raul at once had mentioned Rosalie and the hopes he had once had for their life together.

Emma did not mind hearing Rosalie's name but what she minded was the knife that constantly jabbed into her heart every time she thought of her lord and his love. Maja merely talked about a woman from Raul's past, had she talked of a woman in Raul's present that still would not have given Emma permission to feel envy or jealousy for she was not a true bride to Raul. He was a free man, just as she was a free woman. Then why did it hurt to know that he had wanted to die for Rosalie?

"Do ye not think, now that he is wed, it is not right for Raul to think of her still?" Maja asked.

"Lady Wilbert, one can only control thoughts about the future. The past is embedded in our soul. Try as we might, it cannot be forgotten. And if my lord loved her as ye say, then it should not be forgotten. My lords past is not my concern, it is his."

"But what if he wishes to make his past, his present?" Maja injected another dangerous thought into Emma.

"If his past becomes his present, then Lady Wilbert, his present must become his past." Emma replied.

"Do ye comprehend the weight of yer words, she could become Lady Kinsborough, and ye Emma, what title will ye then hold?" Maja questioned further.

"I, Lady Wilbert, will remain Emma of Rosemund. That title can never be taken from me." Emma replied hoping their conversation would somehow come to an end.

It was the woman in the first bed, whose moan, came as the answer to her prayer. Leaving Maja's side, Emma went over to the woman and stayed with her until she was sure that Maja had dosed off to sleep.

Later when Emma lay down on the pallet and shut her eyes, it was Raul that she heard, calling out, not to her, but to Rosalie.

Winifred saw her mistress restless again during the second night. But tonight, that restlessness forebode ill. Maja had said something to Emma that had shattered Emma's peace of mind. She prayed that her lord would return soon for it was Emma who was now in danger not Lord Wilbert or his keep. The enemy from the father's keep had infiltrated the son's.

Chapter 15

Raul returned from surveying the borders of Wilbert. All was secure. The battle Maja had written about was a skirmish between two warriors over the loss of some sheep, started by their youthful sons. It had been well settled before they had even arrived.

As he rode back to the keep, he wondered at the urgency in Maja's note. He did not want Maja at Kinsborough but he could not understand the need to call his father back in the way it was done.

While he was glad to have escorted his father home, every moment that had passed, his thoughts had been with Emma. Maybe, he thought, I was wrong to leave her behind. Then he laughed to himself. He better get used to being without her, for there would be no Emma when he joined the crusade.

"Raul!" Rowan's voice cut through and held an air of urgency in it.

"Aye Rowan, what is it?" he asked.

"Have ye seen Lady Wilbert since our arrival?" he asked.

"Nay, she did send a message that she was unwell and missed supper." Raul informed Rowan.

"Raul I would check with Lord Wilbert. I have just been informed by my squire that he overheard the lady's maid say that Lady Wilbert rode out after we arrived along with two knights and a maid"

Raul pulled the reigns to stop Daktonian.

"Why would my father not tell us so? Come I needs find out, the truth of it."

With that Raul raced to the keep and straight to his father's side. Lord Wilbert was seated by the window, looking out to his stable.

"Father, is it true, that Ma'am is well and rode out yesterday?" he asked.

"Aye my son, I had a note left from her this morning. She had been unwell with female issues and thought to see Emma for a cure. She did not want us to be concerned so left this note. I would have told ye earlier but it was given to me soon after ye left on patrol" Lord Wilbert said

"Father, Kinsborough was my mother's home and Ma'am was never to enter it. I thought all knew that." Raul was visibly angry.

"Raul, she is my bride. If ye shut the door to her, ye shut the door to me, is that what ye say?" Lord Wilbert said.

"Aye father, if ye come with her that is what I say. Forgive me, I must leave ye in the care of Sir Maximillian and return to Kinsborough at once." Bowing he left. As he walked out of the hall, Rowan and his knights all stood in readiness. He looked at Rowan

"How did ye know?"

"Yer heart was never here My Lord; this has given us cause to return." Rowan grinned.

Raul returned the smile as he lifted himself into the saddle.

"Raul!" a voice called out to him. Turning he saw Maximillian race towards him.

"Sir.." he began.

"I know. Yer father just informed me. Raul this is betwixt us only. We have all tolerated Lady Maja for Lord Bruce's sake. I do not expect ye to do the same for ye have much more to protect. I will say this, let yer bride handle this, in her own way."

"Sir Maximillian, Emma does not see the treachery that I see in Ma'am. If I do not protect her, she will be unable to do so herself. Ma'am knows well how to deceive."

"Raul, ye go to the Order soon, who will protect Emma then. Kinsborough is a mere four hours journey away, how will ye keep Lady Wilbert away forever. Leave Emma to handle this for she, has a long life ahead without a lord, and a keep that will always be a target for many." Maximillian expressed what all felt, secretly even Raul.

Raul was silent. Maximillian was right, who would protect Emma when he was gone. The thought of her at the mercy of Maja and her like, made his blood boil. But to do nothing now was folly. One, he would not forgive himself for.

"Nay Sir Maximillian, Ma'am is treachery personified. I cannot let Emma deal with Ma'am alone, when even my own mother was unable to protect herself." Raul replied.

"I have heard such claims many times from ye, what Raul do ye really say?" Maximillian asked.

"Only one person gained from my mother's death. I ask ye Sir Maximillian, my mother was afraid of heights, then why was she where a fall could kill her?" Raul asked.

Maximillian remained still. Raul spoke of murder. He had heard many murmur questions in the past but had not paid heed, for Maja was not at Wilbert when it happened. But Raul was right in that Lady Christina was terrified of heights but to suspect murder. Surely not!

"Sir Maximillian I plead with ye to remain with my father. See that food and drink is tested before it is given to him. I will return the day I have proof."

"God speed Raul. Fear not for I will remain with Lord Bruce until I have word from ye." Maximillian promised.

"Thank ye, I owe ye much." he bowed with his words

"Nay, ye owe me nothing. Ye brought the joy of a child to my home. Go Raul, but know this, if ye go to Emma's aid now, ye must think again about leaving for the Order." he said

"I need go, for I will never forgive myself if I fail her too." he replied.

Maximillian had the confirmation he had long suspected. Raul blamed himself for failing to protect his mother. Every act of his was his way of punishing himself; every word, a form of retribution.

"Aye maybe ye know more than I." with that Maximillian waved them off.

A second later they were galloping away. Maximillian turned to see Bruce standing at the steps. The sadness he saw on his countenance spoke all that was to be said. With a determined gait he walked toward Bruce. He would remain by Bruce until Raul returned.  He prayed hard that Raul would return soon.

As they rode back, Raul repeated to himself that it was his fault that the snake had entered his keep. The causes of his anger were so inter-mingled that he was unsure as to which was the primary concern -the fact that Maja had dared to enter Kinsborough or that Emma was at the mercy of the witch.

At Kinsborough, with day break the usual activities commenced. Emma's hardest task was keeping Maja out of the keep. Her morning meal was brought to the sick room but how long could Emma keep her away from the great hall. And Maja insisted on following Emma everywhere saying it would give her a chance to talk. Finally deciding that it was impossible to keep walking around outside the keep she suggested they ride out to find some more herbs. It was not a task that Maja found interesting but found the idea of Emma outside the castle and with limited protection an opportunity not to be missed. A riding accident, a fall in the lake or a gentle nudge over the ridge, would be an answer to her prayers.

Peter refused to give his permission for the excursion. Winifred was livid that such an event was to take place.

"Then tell me what I should do, for I cannot keep Lady Wilbert out of the keep much longer." Emma pleaded to both of them, then turning to Peter she asked.

"Sir Peter, ye know my lord well, what would he do if he were in my place?"

"He would ask Lady Wilbert to leave, My Lady." Sir Peter's reply was frank and forth coming.

"Ah there lies the problem. He is the Baron of Kinsborough and can do that, I have no such authority."

"My Lady, ye are the Baron's bride, that is authority enough."

Unable to take the step of asking Maja to leave, Emma prepared to ride out with her to gather herbs.

As the gate was lifted to let them out, the dust storm that rode in brought with it the Baron of Kinsborough. Emma stared unbelievingly at the countenance that emerged through the dust.

If she was shocked, Maja was astonished. Raul was to stay two nights at least, yet there he stood in the bailey of his own keep just one night later.

"Ma'am, I was not aware ye planned to visit Kinsborough, had ye informed me when we met before supper that ye needed my lady's healing, I would have brought her to Wilbert. Had ye said ye were coming here, I would have escorted ye." Raul's words surprised Emma for Maja had spoken of no ailment.

"I thought to acquaint myself with yer bride first, and then intended to seek her aid." Maja lied.

"Ye should be with yer lord Ma'am. It does not speak well when Lord Bruce's bride does not seek his leave before leaving his castle." Raul taunted.

"I did not sneak out. Ye would have all believe that I betrayed my lord by coming to see yer bride. I did no wrong." she remarked.

"Nay Ma'am that is not wrong. Entering my keep without my permission, that ma'am was the wrong." Raul left no one in doubt that he was upset, very upset.

"Raul I am yer father's bride, I do not need permission to enter." she replied.

"Aah Ma'am that is where ye are wrong, this is my castle and all who enter are required to have it. Wilbert is my father's. Wilbert is where ye do not need permission to enter and it is where ye should return." Raul ordered.

"Yer father will not be pleased, I am his lady. I am akin to yer mot.." she screeched.

"DO NOT utter it Ma'am, ye are not her and ye never will be. When the sun rises, I expect ye to be gone."

With that he rode in further, alighted and handed the reins to his squire. Without a backward glance he walked up the steps and disappeared into the keep. Emma had not been acknowledged nor had Peter.

After he left, all stood where there were, transfixed by the exchange that had taken place.

Emma looked in the direction of the hall. What had Maja done that brought out such anger?

Peter looked at Rowan who seemed equally shocked, and raised his shoulders as if to say 'I have no answers either'

Then Sir Peter said "Lady Wilbert it is best ye retire to the sick room, I will escort Lady Emma to the keep" Then turning to Winifred he said, "Stay with Lady Wilbert until I come"

After they had gone he turned to Emma and said "I better go and meet with the Baron unless ye would prefer to incur his wrath first?" he asked.

"Nay, ye have more experience Sir Peter. I will tend to my garden while ye calm down yer lord." She smiled but Peter could see that she was really worried.

As she walked away she added "Mayhaps Sir Peter, I should have done as ye had said."

Peter smiled, but did not word his thoughts.

All outside could hear voices but could not make sense of the words. Unable to bear the tension of not knowing,

Emma went towards the keep. As she neared the great hall she heard Sir Peter speak.

"Raul, yer lady did not permit her to enter. That is my fault. The guards had let Lady Wilbert in. I should have asked her to leave that night itself."

"Why did ye not?" Raul asked.

"I did not know how to evict a woman at night." Peter said.

"Ye chivalry will get ye killed one day." Raul remarked.

"It nearly did, just a short while ago, when the Baron returned." Peter joked. Emma listening outside smiled.

"Peter, ye know my past. Ma'am staying in this keep is like polluting my mother's memory. Ye understand that do ye not?" Raul asked in a softer tone.

"Aye Raul, even ye bride understands that. She lied that the rooms were in repair and took Lady Wilbert out to the sick room. She even stayed in the sick room herself the night, so that Lady Wilbert did not enter ye keep for it was already too late to stop her from entering the castle." Peter explained.

This news took Raul by surprise. He had worried the whole journey back and on reaching Kinsborough he saw Maja and Emma conversing as friends and on the verge of leaving the castle together. The sight made him see red. Already Rosalie had betrayed him for Maja, now Emma was doing the same.

Peter's words made him ashamed that he had deliberately ignored Emma as he entered. Emma's loyalty should always be to him first. That was, the one and only thing he wanted from her. But even as he said it to himself, he knew it was no longer true.

"I apologise to ye for my bad behavior." Raul turned to Peter.

"Ye do not need to Raul. I believe I would have done the same in yer seat" Peter said

Emma hearing them felt great pride in Raul. He was a man who was not ashamed to admit he was wrong and nor was he above himself to apologise for it.

"I will seek Emma out and speak to her" As soon as Emma heard her name she ran  towards the sick room but not having enough time to enter it as Raul had already turned the corner, she hid behind one wall.

Thinking Emma to be in the sick room, Raul walked up to it. On entering he saw Maja seated on the pallet and Winifred clearing away jars.

"Pardon, I thought my bride was here" As he turned to exit, he heard a voice.

Chapter 16

"I know why ye did it." Maja said.

"I do not know what ye refer to ma'am" Raul countered.

"This game ye have made of yer marriage" Maja continued.

Raul looked at Winifred and asked her to leave them for a few moments. When she was gone he said.

"My marriage is no game."

"No game ye say' Maja screeched "Ye have a bride ye picked up on a journey, ye have a bride who does not share yer bed and ye have a partner who has no claim to birth, breeding or beauty. This marriage is offering ye a future with no issues. If that is no game, what is?" she queried

"My marriage is but my concern." he blazed.

"Yer marriage is yer father's concern if it leaves him without an heir. Ye, have deliberately chosen a bride ye will never be attracted to and one who has no inclination of giving ye a child." She said in a raised voice.

"I am his heir, beyond that my father need not worry." Raul spoke up.

"How can he not worry when ye end his line this way." Maja screeched back.

Raul did not bother to reply Maja, instead he turned and walked towards the door.

"Ok, if it is a game ye want to play, a game ye will have. If by the third full moon, yer marriage remains unconsummated then I shall plead with the King to annul yer marriage and give me the task of finding ye a suitable bride. Ye married her for revenge. Ye have achieved that goal. Now let's forget this charade and end yer marriage." she threatened.

"Ye have gone far enough ma'am" Raul screamed "Now stop! Emma is my bride. My bride! And my concern! Our marriage is our matter. I have chosen the bride most suited to my life. Do not interfere yerself, and do not persuade my father to intervene. My father and ye wanted me to marry. I have married. The demand was that I wed, not whom I wed. If ye cannot accept her, it is best ye leave now." with that Raul had given an ultimatum.

"Yer father will disinherit ye." Maja threatened further.

"From what? This is the only place I consider mine. The only place I want. It was given to me by my maternal grandfather. I neither seek anything else nor want it. Disinherit me if ye wish to, but do not, and I repeat, do not interfere in my life, ever again." Raul was on the verge of losing control.

"I did what I thought was best before, I will do what I think is best, again." Maja was not intimidated.

"Best? Best for whom ma'am. Ye ended my betrothal before. I will not let ye end my marriage now. Tonight is the last night ye sleep in my home. Tomorrow ye return to my father's. These gates will never be opened to ye again Ma'am."

Emma heard the door bang just moments before she saw Raul storm past. Luckily she had moved back in time and only relaxed as she heard his footsteps fade away.

Releasing a sign of relief she moved away from the wall.

What was she supposed to do now?  It was true that she had not wanted to wed. It was also true that she had wanted to be free of commitments. She had even wanted to get away from here once. But all that was before. Now for the first time in her life she felt totally safe. Raul made no demands on her and she had a home. She would be a fool to leave it all now. She thought to walk away and forget what she had overheard.

And then she recalled Maja's words. Were they true? Raul had neither denied anything nor refuted any claim. And if Maja carried out the threat of annulment it would cause the greatest of shame and embarrassment for both Raul and her. It was best to end the marriage, to rectify the wrongs and move on. No one was happy with his marriage, not his father, not Maja, and definitely not Raul. She could free everyone and Maja was the key to her escape.

Wiping the tears, that she had not realised she had shed; she walked softly towards the sick room.

Maja was standing facing the window but turned as she heard the door open.

"Ye! What do ye want?" she spoke harshly.

"Yer help Lady Wilbert." Emma whispered.

"My help?" Maja was honestly puzzled.

"When the Baron married me, he saved me from a wretched future. We wed for our own reasons but neither truly wanted to marry. I thought our situation was ideal. He had his freedom and I had mine. But I see now the unfairness of my staying here. The Baron needs a real bride. He needs to secure his future with a son, and I cannot give him that." she explained

"Did ye not think of this before marrying Raul?" Maja's tone reflected her dislike of Emma.

"Nay Lady Wilbert there was no time to think. I was being sold and the Baron won me with his bid...."

"Raul bought ye?" Maja had just been given the weapon she needed, to get this marriage annulled. Continuing in a softer tone she said "That cannot be. Raul had women of great beauty waiting to marry him, families of great standing, wishing to make the alliance with us. Yet he chooses a bride from a sale. Revenge may have been his motive, but to marry one so beneath him. What could he have been thinking?" Maja continued her insults, oblivious to the fact that she was insulting Emma to her face.

When Emma had not replied to her insults, Maja looked at Emma who continued to stand in silence.

"Ye said ye wanted my help, how?" Maja knew she had to grab this opportunity.

"Help me leave this place. Take me with ye when ye leave in the morrow." Emma asked.

"My husband's son will never allow that." Maja replied, but in her mind she knew Emma would no longer remain in the castle to see another sunset.

"The Baron will not know until after I am gone. If ye can get me to The Abbey of St. Mary, I will find help there." She pleaded.

Maja thought over the request and smiled. The solution was presenting itself and she must grab the opportunity while she had the chance.

"I believe it can be done. Raul has asked me to leave and I will do so when the rooster crows. Tonight ye will pretend to be ill and not come down, so no one will wonder at yer not coming to bid me farewell. Ye must come down after we have broken fast. My maid will hide ye amidst my belongings. Once we are outside the gates, ye can ride a steed. Do not take too much with ye." she warned.

"I do not have much ma'am."

"Good. Tell me Emma, Why leave now? Why did ye not leave before?" Maja questioned.

"I had not the means, with which to leave before." she lied.

"Raul may not agree but I think ye have chosen yer path wisely. Raul does not realise it yet but in time he would have come to hate ye. A man needs a beautiful bride, a rich bride and a powerful bride. Ye may have a good heart but not the rest."

"I know Lady Wilbert." was Emma's only reply.

After confirming the arrangement, Emma walked through the door, knowing this would be the last time she would ever walk through her beloved sick room.

As planned Emma feigned illness that night. Raul organised for broth to be sent to her room and made her excuse to his people. Maja retired early as well.

When the meal was over and his knights had retired, Raul came to the room to find Emma asleep. He stood watching her for several minutes and then slowly walked away to his room.

As soon as the door shut, Emma let out a sigh of relief.

She told herself that she was right to correct a wrong. Yet as she lay alone staring at the door Raul had just walked through, she felt completely desolate, once again bereft of the feeling of belonging to a place or a person. But she knew that it was the right thing. The just thing! Raul carried heavy responsibilities on his shoulder. An heir for him could never just be a possibility. An heir, for him, had to be a certainty.

Some hours later, the moon had moved much higher into the night sky but sleep evaded her. Guilt ate at her soul.

She knew of the great wrong she was going to do him, with her departure. The shame of having yer bride, run away! The disgrace of having a marriage ended. Men had killed their wives for lesser wrongs than the one she was going to commit. But of the two wrongs, his marriage to her and the end of it, the first needed to be corrected. Raul must have the chance to marry again and to have his heir. And maybe his betrothed still waited for him to return.

When she was sure that Raul would have fallen into deep slumber, she got out of her bed and collected all her belongings, and tied them up into a bundle. This she hid beneath her bed. Then she lay down on it again and awaited sleep.

She was still looking at the wall, when she realised that dawn had broken, for the sun's rays fell on that very wall reminding her that the moment had come.

When she heard footsteps outside her door she feigned sleep again. She knew it was Raul for there was no knock, before the door opened. She sensed him move towards her bed.

"Emma?" She did not reply

"Emma, it is time to awaken. Ma'am is leaving this morn and if ye are feeling better, ye need to come and bid her farewell. It will be expected." She heard him say, as he gently shook her shoulder.

Emma opened her eyes and turned slowly to find Raul watching her.

"If ye wish it My Lord, I will be there." Emma replied knowing that as soon as he left the room she would send the message that despite her attempts she did not feel well enough to come down.

"It is my wish" he replied

"In that case I best get dressed My Lord." With that Emma arose from the bed.

But the stress of her lie, her sleepless night and the fear of her actions, made her sway. Raul reached out and pushed her back onto the bed.

"Nay, ye are not well enough yet. Stay in bed. I will explain yer absence." Raul spoke in a softer tone

Emma though worried at her dizziness, felt relief. Without having to lie further, she had once again been given her excuse.

Raul left the room appearing worried, though he did not express that in either word or action. Emma crept from the bed and opened the door, just wide enough for her to follow Raul's progress down the corridor. This would be the last time she would see her husband. Unblinking she followed his every step, until he turned the corner. Then she turned and rushed through her morning tasks.

Emma pulled out the bundle. She removed her wedding band and placed it on the table beside her bed. There was no need for a message. Raul would know that she had finally succeeded in her escape.

While everyone sat in the main hall as they broke their fast, Emma boarded the cart and lay down at the back. Maja's belongings where then placed carefully in front so that no part of Emma was visible. A rough cloth was placed over all the boxes and tied down with strong twines. Emma was left in that position for the next half hour until everyone was ready to move.

Emma could see nothing but she knew as soon as Raul came out. Holding her breath she waited while he bid Maja goodbye.

It was a civil goodbye but one that made it clear that Maja was no longer welcome. Emma remained hidden, too scared to even peek out.

As the cart moved through the gate, she held her breath and continued to remain very still. Raul's guards would be on the barbican. Despite the covering any movement would be noticed by them.

Finally she let out a breath of air as the last part of the wheel moved onto rough terrain. It was a sign that they were out of the castle gate. She had escaped. He was free. Yet she found that she was crying, silent tears, painful tears, at a moment when it should have been her time of joy.

She heard Maja's voice as she directed her people "Do not stop until we can no longer see the castle"

They would not have traveled far for she could still hear the movements in the keep, when the earth rumbled with the sound of galloping horses. And Sir Peter's voice boomed through the air.

'In the name of the Baron of Kinsborough, halt at once."

"Keep going" Maja's nervous voice hurried her man.

"Did ye not hear Sir Peter, Ma'am or do ye defy the order?" Raul's voice cut through the air.

"Is something wrong Raul?" Maja tried to keep calm.

"I believe Ma'am, ye have something of mine with ye" Raul replied

Emma let out a small breath. He obviously did not know that she was there. He had come to retrieve a material belonging and wondered what Maja had taken.

"Are ye here to accuse me of theft?" Maja ensured that she sounded offended.

"I am here, to reclaim what is mine" Raul seemed unaffected by Maja's insinuation.

"Let Raul inspect all my belongings. Bring out one box at a time and open it in front of him. I will not have this accusation on me. Bring the first box" she ordered

"That will not be required Ma'am. What is mine is not in yer boxes? Raul replied sternly.

He knew! Emma was now sure of it. But just in case there was a possibility that she was wrong, she remained hidden. Her punishment would not be lessened because she surrendered herself quicker.

"What I have on me belongs to me Raul. I have nothing of yers either in my boxes or on my person, I give ye my oath on this. Yer father will hear of this and he will be most displeased, that his bride, was stopped as a common thief." Maja braver now at the knowledge that her belongings would not be searched.

"I believe, my father, despite his displeasure with me, will be disappointed to know that his son's property is being taken from him, without his son's permission ma'am." Raul replied

"Yer property? And what is that property? Maja queried

"My bride." Raul replied in just two words.

"Is this what all this fuss is about? Yer bride did not have the courtesy to come and bid me goodbye. Mayhaps ye should look for her in her room and let me pass as we have a long journey ahead and I wish to reach yer father before darkness falls." Maja motioned for John to continue.

"Halt there!" Raul shouted. At his words, Sir Rowan rode in front of the steeds and Sir Peter moved to the rear.

John pulled the reins and the cart came to a halt, fear clearly displayed on his countenance.

"Ma'am, only a fool looks for his lost belonging, where it is not going to be found.  What is mine is here with ye. Ye may proceed once I have recovered my property."

Then looking at two of his men, who had quietly moved to his side, he asked them to remove the covering that hid Emma.

Trembling in fear Emma tried to move but found that she was unable. Even when sunlight fell on the cloak covering her she remained still.

"My Lord." one of them addressed Raul. The message was conveyed in those two words. It said, yer bride is here and she attempts to remain hidden. Raul signaled for them to get down from the cart.

"My Lady!" Raul's called out. Silence met his request.

'EMMA! He yelled, when there continued to be no response.

Raul rode around the carriage, wondering why Emma maintained the silence. She must know that she had been found out and her attempt was over. Her onward journey now consisted of a walk back into the keep.

"Emma, no one will be allowed to leave while ye remain in the cart. And by staying there longer ye are increasing the punishment both yer maids will receive for failing in their duty to protect ye. Do ye wish that to happen?" he issued the threat he knew would work.

Raul banked on Emma's inability to see another suffer, and though neither Winifred nor Mary, would ever be held responsible, he used the threat he knew would achieve the result and mentally began to count the numbers.

Emma had not thought of this one repercussion. How could she have been so stupid as to have put the lives of others in jeopardy? Slowly she rose, lifting the cloak and letting it fall.

"She begged me to take her. Ask her Raul. If was her plan, I just agreed to assist a woman who made it very clear that she wished to leave ye." Maja took great delight in her statement.

Emma saw anger flicker across Raul's face at Maja's word. The look was also given to her. Sir Peter glanced accusingly and the people looked at her with distrust. She had let them all down. Would her noble intentions ever be enough to gain their forgiveness?

"Please get down from the cart." Raul addressed Emma, ignoring Maja's outburst.

Emma slowly moved to the edge of the cart. It was too high for her to jump and she wavered there for a moment.

As she hesitated, she noted that Sir Peter moved to aid her but was stopped by Raul.

"She climbed up onto the cart without our aid, Sir Peter, I am sure she can manage climbing down on her own" Raul's eyes had not wavered from hers.

Emma sat down and swung her legs over the edge, careful to ensure that not even her ankle was seen beneath her gown. The crowd had formed a circle and she realised that by trying to leave their Lord, she had lost their regard. She would never have their trust again but after the spectacle they were witnessing, she would never have their respect either. Her tears blurred her vision, long enough for Raul to bring his stead by her side. Soon he had alighted and was standing in front of her.

Lifting her chin with his thumb he whispered "Ye broke yer word when ye stepped outside the gate. I am no longer bound by my promise. Ye no longer protected by yers."

With that he placed his hand on her waist and lowered her to the floor. He waited until she had become steady on her feet and then removed his hands.

'Sir Peter, please escort My Lady to the keep." Raul addressed his friend, without once taking his gaze away from Emma

"How can ye want her to remain here after the insult she has just given ye? Yer wedded bride just tried to escape from yer castle. She asked me to take her away. Ask her yerself, if ye do not believe me!" Maja screeched hoping to break Raul's stare.

Raul's eyes remained steadfast on Emma, and without even blinking, he addressed Emma ensuring that his voice was loud and audible to all, even in the keep. "Tell me My Lady, did ye decide to leave before or after ye heard my conversation with Ma'am yesterday, when, she threatened to get our marriage annulled?"

Silence fell across the crowds. Sir Peter and Sir Rowan smiled. With one stone Raul had achieved two goals -

redeemed Emma in the eyes of his people and proclaimed Maja as the maker of trouble.

Emma could not look away from Raul either. Her fear was palpable. Her shame visible!

In a mere whisper she replied "I did what I thought was going to be for the best, My Lord."

If her voice was a whisper, Raul was an explosion "Best for whom My Lady?"

Emma jumped 'I have nothing to offer the Baron of Kinsborough. That bundle is all I have in the world."

Raul ran his fingers through his hair in frustration. This was not the answer he had wished to hear.

"I am asking ye again, did ye, decide to leave, before or after ye heard my conversation with Ma'am yesterday, when she threatened to get our marriage annulled?"

Raul's voice once again carried across the keep.

"After My Lord." she whispered back.

"I do not think Ma'am heard ye My Lady. Please raise yer voice so that all may hear yer reply." Raul continued.

Emma raised her voice to the loudest she could and replied "After, My Lord."

Raul let out the breath he had been holding back.

"Ye may go back to the keep My Lady. Sir Peter will escort ye to yer room and stay guard until I arrive." then Raul looked at Sir Peter

"No one goes into My Lady's room, nor does anyone leave it."

Sir Peter alighted and handing over the reins to his squire, he bowed to Emma and actioned for her to lead, with the word 'My Lady"

Emma brushed away the tears that had escaped, and began to follow Sir Peter, when she remembered that she needed to bid Maja goodbye. As she turned she found that Raul was still looking in her direction. As if guessing her intention he said, "Yer goodbye can be said from the distance at which ye stand."

If she needed any proof that he no longer trusted her, she had got it with those words. She had lost much, in her attempt to give him all.

"I wish ye a safe journey Lady Wilbert" Emma worded

Ignoring Emma, Maja addressed Raul instead "The least ye can do is tell me, how ye knew and if ye already knew, why did ye wait until we had left the castle to stop us?"

Raul smiled to himself, before turning his icy cold gaze towards Maja, "Have ye not heard Ma'am, even walls have ears."

"Then why let us get this far?" Maja continued with her question. It was one that played on Emma's mind too.

"Because until ye past the gate, My Lady would still have been on Kinsborough soil" Was Raul's only reply

"I still remain perplexed. What difference does that make?" Maja queried.

Raul once again looked at Emma and knew that she had understood the implication. In taking that one step outside the gate, she had broken her promise and nullified his.

Then addressing Emma he said "Sir Peter is waiting". Emma did not need to remain any longer. Maja had ignored her farewell. Raul no longer wanted her presence. Turning she walked towards the keep.

Raul watched a second more before turning to Maja. By now Sir Rowan had moved to Raul's side. And Raul's knights had taken defensive positions.

"Ma'am, no one, but no one, will take what is mine ever again. Emma is mine. Come betwixt us once more and ye will make a son, an enemy of even his father." Maja shivered at his words and his frozen stare.

"Ye are not yer father's son." Maja hit back

"That Ma'am, can be a possibility, but what is certain, is that, I am not yers." Raul returned the favour.

"Keep her then, Raul and regret it. Look at her Raul. She is not worthy of ye."

"MA'AM" Raul roared

"Oh, save yer grunts for someone else. My warning still stands. Three months and if things remain the same here,

I will get yer marriage annulled. The law is on my side, and ye know it Raul. Ye know it well."

"Leave Ma'am and know ye are never welcome back." with that Raul climbed onto his destrier. Unprompted Daktonian trotted back into the castle.

Sir Rowan followed his lord, but unlike Raul, Rowan stopped on reaching the gate, turned and stood guard, ensuring that Maja continued on her journey away from the castle.

Fuming at her disappointment, Maja was aided onto her steed and moments later rode away. Sir Rowan watched until the dust no longer rose in their wake, then turned his steed and rode in. While he too was glad to see the last of Maja, he was also aware of the great enemy his lord had just made. They would have to be vigilant, for a wounded animal waits to attack. Maja's ego had been hurt and she also had many friends in the king's court, friends that one would not want to cross paths with.

The gate was shut as soon as the last of Raul's men were within its safety. As the gate was lowered, Raul began his climb up to Emma's room.

Chapter 17

Upstairs Emma walked the length of her room. Sir Peter had not stepped into it but his presence outside her room was announced with each cough and with each footstep he took as he paced outside.

There were only two exits to her room. One was guarded by Sir Peter. The other led to the parapet outside her room. That parapet followed along the four rooms and connected to Raul's room at the end and that would lead her back to where Sir Peter stood. The only other option was to jump off the parapet, but there was no escape via that route either for there was a 20 feet fall to the lower wall walk.

As she heard a second set of footsteps outside her door, her heart began to pound. She knew Raul was already there for no other person would have dared to come up after Raul had made his instructions clear. She dreaded to think what would happen next. The law gave him the right to punish her and the people of Kinsborough would never question his action. She did not want to think further. The dungeon, whipping, torture, were the words that created fear, for she had experienced all before and knew of the suffering each would bring. She recalled his words 'ye are no longer protected by yers." What had he meant by that? Did he plan to annul the marriage? Did he plan to send her away? But if that were the case then why had he not let her escape? And why if he knew she was leaving had he let her go past the gate before preventing her departure. The only thing that made sense was that he wanted to punish her and now he was given the reason to throw her in the dungeon. That was her guardian's answer when she opposed him. What she had done now was worse and would never be accepted by any wedded lord much less a Baron of Raul's standing.

Outside the door Sir Peter, watched apprehensively as his lord stormed up the steps. Even as a prisoner, when the guards tortured and abused Raul almost on a daily basis, Sir Peter had never seen him angry. For the first time in all the years that he had known Raul, he saw him loose control. The disappointment he had shown on his face when he had walked into Emma's room and found it empty, save for her wedding ring. The anger he had shown when he had seen Emma climb into the cart and then aid Maja's maid. And the sheer violence in his words, when Maja had spoken of Emma's desire to leave.

Everyone knew of the strange arrangement betwixt Raul and his bride. In time everyone had come to accept their unusual marriage. If their Lord was accepting of his situation, they would be too. But the male honour can take only so much. To find his bride, the lady of the keep, sneaking out of the castle, with of all people, his step-mother, must have seen the end of the baron's patience. Now he feared for the lady. As a knight he would try and defend his lady but Raul as her wedded husband had the power to do as he wished and they lived in an age when the law gave the husband all the power in the world.

"My Lord, would it be better if ye went to our lady, after yer anger has abated?" Sir Peter voiced as he saw Raul reach him.

"Do ye question a husband's judgement, Peter?" Raul spoke back.

"Never Raul, but for the first time I see my friend hurt like a man, rage like a man. Our lady .." Peter spoke

"I too see a friend waver between his loyalties as a friend and as a knight. My bride is my concern. Only mine! See that we are not disturbed." Laying a hand over Peter's shoulder, he pulled open the door and stepped in. A moment later the door closed behind Raul shutting out Sir Peter.

Just then Winifred walked up to Peter. "Do not worry Sir Peter, our lord, will not hurt our lady. He has just made an enemy of his own father for her. It is but right, that he ensure her safety. Ye too must see that my lady's security lies in her remaining within the walls of this castle. Our lord has made a powerful enemy in Lady Wilbert. If our lady is to be kept safe, she must never endanger herself again by leaving this keep."

Sir Peter agreed with all Winifred said, but still he feared Raul's anger. During a mortal combat, he had seen Raul break the neck of a battle hardened warrior with one jerk. His lady would not stand a chance if Raul resorted to violence. While he acknowledged that Raul had never hit a woman before, he had never exhibited such anger before either.

And his own position now was an unenviable one, as a knight he would have to defend his lady's honour yet with that very act, he would be going against his lord and the code of chivalry, for the two codes would clash with the one event.

He walked some distance away and leaning against a pillar, looked into the distant horizon. Winifred went and seated herself at the first step of the stairwell.

Inside Emma watched as Raul shut the door and moved into the room. He stood several paces from her and once again simply watched her. No words, no movements, just an unwavering glare.

Finally Emma could take the silence no longer and spoke first "My Lord, I did what was for the best."

"And again I ask, best for whom?" Raul repeated his earlier question

"For ye, My Lord! For the people of Kinsborough too! Ma'am was right in saying Kinsborough needs an heir. And ye too My Lord need a true bride" Emma expounded.

"Well since ye were so concerned for my happiness, ye can provide me with both."

As Raul uttered the word he saw Emma turn deathly pale.

"Ye promised My Lord." She whispered back

"Why is my promise of greater value than yers, My Lady? And as I said before, when ye stepped outside the castle, ye broke yer promise. At that moment our pact ended. Our promises ended." he articulated.

"A Lord's promise is forever. A knight's must never be broken." she reminded.

"A Lady must honour her word. A bride must keep steadfast and loyal." he countered.

"My honour is in that, I did what I thought would be right for ye and yer people. My loyalty to ye remains unquestionable." she defended herself.

"Then where is yer wedding ring? Or are ye loyal in thought only?" he countered

"I was not capable of the commitment, it asked." she said in a low voice.

"Did I ask of ye what ye seem to think the ring did?" Raul questioned.

"In time it would be expected!"

"Do ye not think that yer Abbey would ask for commitments?" he continued.

"Yes My Lord, but the commitment it would ask of me, was one that I was willing to give." she replied

"Ye break yer holy vows and ye dishonor yer commitment to our marriage, yet ye believe ye will honour yer vows to the church." he said exasperatedly.

"I have broken no vow My Lord. We live as we agreed before we wed." she objected.

Raul did what he always did when he felt frustrated. He combed his fingers through his hair. An act, that seemed to calm him down.

"How was it right to leave yer husband without his knowledge, without his permission and without a farewell. A wedding ring left on a table, was a coward's way of exiting." he accused.

"And marrying a woman when ye did not want a bride, just because yer father wanted ye to wed, is that not a coward's way out too?" Her accusation was to match his.

"I did not marry because I feared my father. I married to best him and then anger him." with his words he confirmed Maja's claim. That was all that Emma needed to hear.

"I know My Lord, I was told all, this night before. Like ye My Lord, I had no wish to wed. Ye promised me security. Ye promised me freedom. It was two things I much desired. And like ye My Lord, I accepted to wed for my own selfish reason. I did not condemn yer reasons to wed then, I do not condemn yer reasons for wedding me now. But the rules we set, have changed and it asks from both was neither wanted to give. By leaving I was making the path clear for both of us." she clarified.

"Ye are right to say, I did not want to marry. But our marriage has made me understand, that marriage too has much to give a person and his home. I would have what other wedded couples have. Companionship, children and lo.." Raul was not allowed to finish his sentence.

By the time he had uttered those words, Emma had moved swiftly and climbed over the parapet wall. Too late Raul realised her intention and shouted for Winifred and Peter. The door opened and Winifred entered but Peter was not to be seen.

"My Lady!" Winifred screamed

Emma looked at Winifred. She knew what Winifred must be thinking. The same as what everyone else would think. If she could, she would save Raul from those thoughts but not if she was going to be forced into a real marriage. It was not for her and would never be for her. She had to make him understand.

Raul for the first time in his entire life was left speechless. To know that his bride so disliked the thought of a true wedded life with him that she would give up her life before accepting it, was a thought that pained him deeply. Too deeply for a man who once claimed that he never wanted to love again. When Rosalie was lost to him he thought he had been heartbroken but he realised now what heartbroken really meant, as he watched his bride stand on the rampart just inches from death, yet preferring it, to life with him.

"Emma, stop!" he pleaded. He could not endure to see another lifeless body after a fall. His mother's body was one too many already.

"Winifred, tell everyone I choose this path for my own failings, not my lord's." Emma addressed Winifred instead.

"Emma, if ye wish us to live as we have so far, then I accept it, but pray get down from there." Raul pleaded again

"Only if ye give me yer oath that ye will not make me move into yer room." she bargained

The thought of ending her life seemed brave when she first ran toward the parapet but now standing just moments away from a twenty feet fall, it did not seem brave at all. What foolishness prevailed to make her act as such? She, who was terrified of heights.

"Ye have my word." Raul hastily agreed.

Emma swayed, more from relief than fear but it was enough to let out a startled sound from both Raul and Winifred.

At that moment Emma heard the words "My Lady?" uttered behind her. It was Sir Peter's voice and it sounded very close. Just as she turned to look towards Sir Peter, she was plucked off the parapet and held within the strong grip of her lord's arms. His heart was racing as Athena's did after a long gallop.

When would things ever go her way? A moment's lapse of concentration and she had gone and ruined the power she had to bargain for more. She was going to ask him to annul the marriage before Maja took matters into her hand. Now trapped again, her demands would amount to nothing.

The grip around her was still strong, yet she felt his arms quiver. She feared it symbolised his rage. She tried to break away only to find his grip had tightened further.

She missed the look of relief Peter and Raul shared. She missed the tension leave Winifred's face. So at Raul's next words, her apprehension grew ten folds.

"Peter, see that this door is bolted from the inside and nailed shut from the outside. And ask the blacksmith to embed metal rods into the window frame so no one can go through them, not even a child." With that, Raul walked Emma inside.

Shocked at his command, Emma, knew herself now truly imprisoned. She tried once more to break free and once again the grip tightened.

She also heard the door shut behind her. A heavy object seemed to have been dragged against it and then footsteps faded away.

Once the door had been secured, Raul released her arm.

"My Lady, I do not make agreements while being held to ransom. That was the first time and the last, ye will ever do that, do ye understand me?"

"Aye My Lord." came Emma's soft reply.

"Winifred please see to yer duties. I will send for ye when ye are needed. And Winifred, ye are to see that yer lady is henceforth never left alone." he commanded

Winifred glanced at Emma and then replied "Yes My Lord. We will all have to be vigilant. Yer bride is a flighty one." Laughing she walked away towards the stairwell.

"Now let me hear the rest of yer demands, for I am sure there was more." Raul offered

"Aye My Lord, there is but one more." she replied

"Well, what is it?" he demanded through a controlled voice.

"I want an annulment, My Lord" she replied. Silence met her words.

"For what purpose?" he questioned after several moments.

"To save us the embarrassment, before one is demanded by the king. So ye My Lord can marry again and have yer heir. And so I can live my life free of any expectations."

"There is none born on this earth of whom there are no expectations. Why should ye have the privilege that the rest of us mortals do not have?" he questioned

"Ye My Lord ran away from yers. I believe My Lord, that I should be given the allowance that ye gave yerself." was her reply

"But I did not run away from mine. I married as was expected of me." Raul put in

"I know My Lord, ye married me, so that ye could avoid all other expectations." she said

"Just as ye changed my mind about marriage, ye have also changed my mind about an heir. I will fulfill that expectation too" Raul added

"But ... ye promised me freedom, and ye gave me yer word that ye would honour my wish." Emma uttered fearfully.

"My promise was linked to yers. When ye broke yers, I was freed of mine." he noted.

"Then My Lord, at the first chance I get, I will leave, even if I have to try jumping again." Emma threatened with words she had not the courage to follow through with.

Raul was silent. He never wanted to face what he had just done. He never wanted to spend a moment wondering if Emma was risking her life in another foolish attempt to escape. He wanted much more from his marriage now but he was not going to demand it or take it from an unwilling bride.

After what seemed an eternity, he said "If I give ye my word that I will make no demand of ye, will ye promise me and this time abide by that promise, that ye will never leave this castle alone nor attempt this foolishness again?" he asked

"And what of an annulment?" she queried.

"I cannot give ye that." were Raul's uncompromising words.

"What if the king demands it?" she asked.

"The king will never make that demand of ye." he said
with confidence.

"How can ye be so certain My Lord? Our marriage fulfills
the one condition for an annulment." she added

"Because, the king knows of my desire, to join the Order
of the Templar It is a monastic order that recruits knights
who wish to serve the Lord and fight for His cause. My
father's demand was going to make it impossible to
follow my dream. But then ye came into my life, a bride
who wanted freedom just as much as I. A married man
may be granted entrance to the Order, if his bride gives
him permission. Since ye do not want a true wedded life,
the king and the Order will have no objection to my
becoming a Templar Knight. That, My Lady, should grant
ye, yer wish as well. Ye can continue to have yer freedom
and ye can retain my name and protection." he finally
told all.

Emma was stunned to hear this declaration. A Templar
Knight, promised to the Order with vows of chastity and
service. A life dedicated to war in the name of the Lord. A
life that in all likelihood would one day be sacrificed in a
foreign land, at the hands, of a foreign enemy. Another
foolish man wanting to walk on the path of righteousness
only to finally become a martyr, and like others before
him, paying no heed to the misery they bring to the lives
of their women -their mothers, wives and sisters! Just as
her brother had done! His desire to be a Templar Knight

had not only cost him his life, but it had also taken from her, a beloved brother and everything, including her home and happiness.

Raul noted the varied emotions passing over her countenance. She remained pensive.

"I would have thought this tiding would have made ye glad. Ye will be rid of me for years at a time and even when I return, I will be under the care of the healers. That duty too, will not be expected of ye." Raul spoke

"The path ye have chosen in life does little to relieve my fears, My Lord." She replied.

"And why is that?" he quizzed.

"Do ye know what happens to the women when their men are gone to battle or are killed? They are made wards to another man. If none exist in their family or if they are not married, they are made wards to the first male relative. If they too are not there, then the king chooses anyone he believes acceptable. We are not asked if his decision is right. We are not ensured protection from those appointed to guard us. If ye go to battle, if ye die, I will be passed as ward to another or as bride to one our sire chooses. That is not the future I want My Lord. I wish for an annulment and I ask yer permission to proceed to the Abbey." she said

"The king intervenes in matters to do with noble households. How is it that ye fear such a fate for yerself when as a mere maid, ye would know that yer future will be of no consequence to the king? Ye have no land or coin for him to worry about." Raul diverted his query

"My Lord, I saw what happened to my lady. In my matter, as yer bride, yer father will decide my fate. And his bride will help him. I believe My Lord, ye place me at the gates of hell, if ye chose yer path and do not request the annulment I seek." she pleaded.

"An annulment is no longer an alternative for ye. As a lord's bride, if our marriage is annulled ye will be married to another. Maja will see to it, so that ye can never be a threat to her again. Her only dislike of ye is that ye prevent her niece, from being called the Lady of Kinsborough." Raul revealed another truth.

Emma was silent. So this was why Maja was such a willing partner. She had not thought of the outcome that Raul spoke of either. In light of this news, accepting Raul's offer may be the best course for her. At least until a better option arose. For the moment she was being offered security but was it going to come at a cost that would be too high to pay?

"And what of the lady's threat?" she questioned

"We have three months. I will meet with our king and express my desire to join the order now. I believe he will not approve of an annulment. The Order needs new members. King Richard plans his next crusade. He will need coins and he will need a sword arm. I will bring him both. My father and his bride will never be a threat to ye as long as ye stay within the castle and as long as ye carry my name." Raul said in the hope of giving her assurance.

Again Raul saw a kaleidoscope of emotions play on her face, there was even sadness but not once did she ask him to change his plan. Not once did she request him to stay back at Kinsborough. Instead, when she spoke, her voice was even and her words unaffected.

"Ye have planned well My Lord but ye forget Kinsborough! What barren future do ye plan for her?" her blunt questioning surprised him.

Raul remained silent. Kinsborough! His mother's home was never far from his heart. It was the only reason why he had not applied to the Order with Peter. He had been more than happy to take the vow of chastity. It was the thought of giving up Kinsborough that had been eating at his soul. And then he had found Emma. What would she feel to know that he had hoped that she would remain the lady of Kinsborough while he was away? Sir Rowan would protect the castle, and his bride would protect it against any claim. But after her attempt to escape he was no longer sure that his lady would welcome this 'expectation'.

'Kinsborough chooses its own Lord. It chose me and after me, it will choose another." was all he said. After another silent moment passed he continued, "At this moment Kinsborough's future is not important, ours is. Do I have yer word that ye will not attempt to escape from

Kinsborough ever again? And do I have yer word that ye will not seek an annulment?"

"Ye have much to lose by asking of me, those two vows. I have much to gain by the giving of my word." She debated for him.

"Then give it freely, for in truth I am happy with my lot." His words were spoken with sincerity.

"And ye will not ask me to move out or leave this room again either?"

"Ah, we are back to that. Ye have my word." Raul pledged with a smile.

"Then I give ye mine My Lord. I will not escape from Kinsborough and I will not seek the annulment." With these words Emma, pledged herself one more time.

Raul released a deep breath. He would still ask vigilance from his guards, but as she uttered those words, he felt a joy he had not felt in a long while. She belonged at Kinsborough. And even though she fought the truth, she belonged to him.

"I need to go and assure everyone that all is well and their lady is still alive and willingly stays at Kinsborough. I will come back for ye in a short while. They will want an assurance from ye too." then Raul opened the door and called for Winifred.

A minute later Winifred entered Emma's room.

"Winifred I will send for men to help ye. As My Lady will not move into my room I have no option but to move into hers"

"But My Lord, ye promised!" Emma's voice rose as she uttered the words.

"Again My Lady, I keep my word. Did ye not ask, only, that ye not be forced to move out of yer room?" he asked raising an eyebrow.

"Yes My Lord, but..."

"Winifred ye heard yer lady, she only objects to moving there, she had not expressed an objection to me, moving here." And with that he was gone, his twinkling eyes, only seen by Winifred.

As soon as Raul left, a guard came and took his position outside her door and the second remained at the top of the stairwell.

Pretending anger she really did not feel, she asked Winifred "Do ye see how the Baron breaks his pledge?"

"My Lady after the fright ye just gave all of us, ye are lucky our lord gives ye such concessions. Another husband would not have asked yer promise; he would have demanded yer obedience. My Lady was wise in her choice of a husband." She ended with a laugh.

And then in a more serious tone she added "When ye swayed on the parapet, we thought we had lost ye. My heart is an old one now, pray My Lady, do not frighten it so."

"Pardon Winifred, it was but a ruse. Truly I would not have jumped. I am mortally scared of heights. I ensured that my feet were firm on the rampart."

'My Lady even the best, are prone to accidents." Winifred commented, then after a moment added "My late mistress was afraid of heights too. My late mistress, fell to her death."

Emma now understood why Raul had panicked. She also realised that she had not caused him to panic; it was the memory of a past that still haunted the Baron. To lighten the air she decided to bring humour into their conversation.

"That would have served yer lord well. He would be free of a bride." Emma smiled

"That would have served my lord well, had he wanted to be free of a bride." Winifred corrected.

"He informed me himself, he had wished, never to marry." Emma added.

"That was before My Lady. That was before." Winifred said in a lower tone.

Emma did not get the chance to ask what Winifred meant, for the men arrived to help move the beds. Emma's single bed was removed to one side and Raul's larger bed was brought in. The room next to Emma's was opened up and his armour, hauberk, sword and other weapons were placed there. The door was then bolted from the outside.

As Emma watched the movements, she thought of her conversation with Raul. A lot had just been offered to her in the form of security and status, yet it brought with it the sad knowledge that she would someday lose one more person she loved, and ironically once again it would be to the crusades that promised protection for all.

Love, had she just said love. Emma stilled at the new found knowledge. This would not do at all. Her husband wanted to become a Templar Knight. She herself was seeking freedom. Things had been good between them. Theirs would have been a happy marriage, one of companionship and trust. Now all that had changed. In moments, she had discovered she loved her lord; in moments she discovered he had always planned to leave her.

"My Lady" Winifred repeated herself "Is there need for concern?"

"Nay Winifred, all is, as it was meant to be." With that Emma moved out of the way of the men now carrying in a wooden barrel.

"Place that in the corner." Winifred instructed them while Emma looked on in confusion. She had used this bath soon after her wedding but had not thought it was movable.

"The bath, My Lady." Winifred replied on seeing Emma's confused look.

"My Lord is working on a new machine that will pull the water up, so it will no longer be necessary to carry the pails along the stairwell. He saw it in an Amir's home in the Holy Land."

"Winifred, has the baron ever spoken to ye of his time in the Holy Land?" Emma felt the need to ask.

"Nay My Lady, but what I saw of him, when they carried him home, told me all I needed to know. Even after four months of healing, he came broken and bent. The deep gashes took a long time to heal and his muscles took an even longer time to regain their strength."

"Yet he would go again?" Emma asked

"Some of us My Lady would live well. Some, My Lady, would fight well. Yer husband is a knight first and a man next."

"Even if being a knight will one day see him killed?" she asked in a somber tone.

"The day ye first came here, My Lady, my lord's garments were sprayed with blood. Had he not been a knight, trained in warfare, pledged to chivalry, ye would be a captive of those men, that blood on his garment would have been his own and my lord, would be a memory. Every time my lord trains for battle, my heart aches, but I know too, it is what keeps our baron alive and Kinsborough and its people safe." Winifred explained.

"Kinsborough is safe when yer lord is here. When he has gone to war again, who will then keep Kinsborough safe?" Emma asked. It was often that holdings were usurped by others, while the lords were away in battle.

"Ye will, My Lady." Came Winifred's unhesitant response.

"I am a mere woman not trained in the use of weapons. How will I defend a castle?" Emma questioned in shock.

"As my lord's lady bride, ye carry a greater strength than ye know. Did ye not see outside My Lady, the relief that came over the people when they realised that ye were leaving because of Maja's threat to get ye marriage annulled? And did ye not witness the joy when they knew that ye were not going to leave at all? Ye are our lady now, and every knight will give his life before they let any harm come to ye."

Misty eyed, Emma looked at Winifred.

"They will die for me, yet they let their lord, go to his death?" Emma asked.

"We let him go My Lady, against our will, for none have the power to stop him. Ye My Lady, are the only one, the baron, has given that power to."

"I understand ye not, Winifred?" Emma questioned.

"My Lady, if ye refuse to give yer permission, our lord will not be permitted to join the order." Winifred provided.

"Nay Winifred, if he stays, he must do so, because he wishes it. Of all the women in the world, he chose to wed me so he may have the freedom to go. I cannot make that sacrifice be in vain."

Winifred could say nothing after that and Emma had no more to add. A silence prevailed in the room that was broken some moments later when Raul approached them.

"My Lady, the people of Kinsborough wish to see ye. I believe they too seek an assurance that ye will not leave them again." In that statement Raul also wanted the confirmation that she had not changed her mind.

"My Lord, ye will farewell yer freedom, if ye lead me down the stairs." she warned.

Raul looked at Emma a moment. As answer, Raul walked down the first two steps, then turning he extended his arm and offered her his hand. As she placed her fingers over his palm, his, tightened over hers. And in that moment Emma knew Kinsborough was now her future and its Lord, her destiny. And she had best savour the time she had with him before he too left on the king's mission. Just as her father had done! Just as her brother did!

Carefully they descended the steps and moved toward the great hall. Winifred remained behind for the men had already begun to seal the door leading to the parapet.

"My Lord that is no longer necessary." she remarked as the men hammered the nails into the wooden planks over the door.

"My Lady ye have a way with surprises." Raul smiled, hiding the fact that while the door was being sealed, it was not a permanent move and that should there be a need to escape it could be pushed open by Raul or his knights.

Chapter 18

During the next month, both took extra care not to reveal their true feelings for each other. Instead as perfect friends they looked to the needs of Kinsborough and its people.

Emma continued to work on the herb garden and the vegetable patch, and by the end of that month the vegetable patch had already delivered its first harvest. The fruit trees that included apple, peaches and pears were also planted and she called the area her fruit land.

During the course of the next month, they worked as a true team. He dealt with the administration and safety of Kinsborough, and she looked after the domestic and social needs of the castle.

And every night, after supper, they would stroll on the wall walk. Each evening they would discuss a new topic, and Raul became more and more bewildered at her extensive grasp of politics and ways of the world, especially within the court.

By the end of the month, Raul was certain of several facts, Emma was not only a lady, but she had also looked after the running of a large castle. What he now had to find out was if she ran it as a daughter, sister or bride?

He enjoyed their conversation by day and at night he slept in her room comforted by her steady breathing as she slept. It was however, no secret that their relationship would never give the people their next 'Baron'.

It was a knowledge that gave the people no happiness especially when all felt, their lord and lady, were otherwise so perfectly suited. They hoped for a miracle but all knew the chance of it was slim. Their lord prepared to join the crusade and God surely would not be that merciful as to spare their lord from His very own cause.

The next few weeks saw the same conditions prevail except where the sick room was concerned. There, progress occurred in leaps and bounds. By the end of the month a long hall stood that could easily sleep twenty people. A medicine room was separated with tapestries and resembled the room she had set up for Lord Bruce. In that area the physician treated the sick and there they kept their herbal concoctions. Even Raul had to admit, what stood before him was a piece of marvel.

And what truly amazed him was that not only had the building taken shape but Emma had trained three other women so that they too could help nurse the sick back to health.

Seeing, her truly happy with her work and her life at Kinsborough, Raul yielded, and gave her full freedom to roam the castle. She was even given permission to go and search for her herbs and plants with the physician and at least two other knights. This offer she gladly accepted. He did join her whenever he could but with the minor skirmishes increasing in numbers over the borders of

Kinsborough, his attention was taken up with patrol duty and the training of his men.

A couple of moons later, came Emma's greatest test. A babe of just 10 moons, slipped from her mother's arms and fell down a flight of steps. For an older child, a mere six steps would not have caused as much injury as it did to the little babe. Raul was in the bailey when a knight ran past him asking for the lady. It was the first time a knight of his had ignored his presence. Curious at this show of disrespect, Raul had turned and followed the knight to find him in the sick room, weeping as a babe himself, as Emma held firm to a howling infant as it lay on a raised pallet. The physician was examining the child, but even before the physician spoke, Raul heard Emma say, 'I think she has a break in her arm, would I be right?" she queried.

"Yes My Lady, that seems to be the main concern but she also has many bruises."

"I have witnessed other children who had a break treated by our physician. The physician pulled the arm apart and then pushed the bones together. He then bound the arm tightly with three sticks of wood so the bone would remain straight.  Have ye done such before?"

"Nay My Lady, but I have seen it done. And it must be tried for she is too young to be made a cripple for life." he remarked.

"That will kill my babe." the father cried.

"Leaving her with the break will hurt her more and if it causes an infection it will poison her blood. If we leave it alone it might heal but she will never be able to use that hand properly."

"But the pain will kill her." the father cried again.

"Nay Sir, I will give her the juice of the poppy seed. Only a wee bit for she is very young. It will make her sleep while we fix her arm." Emma added.

"And My Lady, ye will stay with her all the while?" pleaded the man.

"I would not leave her side for a moment sir. I give ye my oath." she pledged.

"Then My Lady, I leave my babe in yer care for I will not be able to witness her pain." he noted.

"My Lord is training with the knights, why do ye not go and watch them. I will send word when we are done." She suggested.

"Nay lady, I will wait outside this room. Please do not let her die, My Lady, do not let her die." He cried.

"We have a good physician, but we could do with yer prayers as well." she said.

"Anthony, I will sit with ye while they tend to yer babe." Raul's voice came as a relief to all. Anthony could do with the Baron's company and Emma was glad to know that he was near in case they needed his help. The physician too had worried how Lady Emma would bear the task ahead.

As Anthony went to kiss his child, Raul came by Emma "And will ye be able to cope with it? If ye like, I can assist the physician instead of ye." He offered.

"I have done it before" she said and then hastily added "there were many children in My Lady's keep and they took turns in having a break."

"Then I will wait with Anthony, call me if ye need aid." he said.

"It is best Anthony goes out now My Lord." she commented as she saw the babe's eyes flutter.

As the men left the area, Emma went near the little girl. The infusion of poppy seeds was working for clearly she could not keep her eyes open any longer.

The physician gave her another few minutes before he set about correcting her bone and then supported her arms with wooden sticks which he bound tightly with cloth and twine.

Once he was sure the bone would not move, he left Emma to care for the babe and he went to look at another child who waited in the great hall.

Anthony came in for a few minutes, but found the sight of his own daughter tied up so distressing he left. Raul walked with him, offering support, amazed the knight who fought so valiantly in battle could not bear to see his child in pain. He wondered what he would have done in Anthony's place and knew he would never have left his child, no matter how heartbreaking the scene had been.

As soon as they left, Emma took her seat next to the pallet. It was going to be a long wait but she did not mind, for it was important that the babe sleep through the initial pain. As far as Emma was concerned the longer the child slept, the better.

Raul came in an hour later to find that Emma had not moved. The babe had begun to stir and she was gently stoking its other arm. Raul had almost reached their side and yet, Emma was unaware of his presence. Deeply engrossed she continued to look at the babe. When she wiped her eyes, Raul realised that Emma was weeping.

"Emma, is the babe alright?" he asked.

"Aye My Lord." she replied without turning.

"Yet ye weep?" he asked.

"She is too little My Lord to suffer as she does." Emma's voice was barely a whisper.

"It is good she is little, she will not remember this pain." he replied.

"Aye My Lord, but at this moment, she suffers for no fault of hers." she remarked.

Raul decided to remain silent in response. It took Emma several moments to compose herself. At one point she noted that Raul reached towards her and then having second thoughts pulled his hand back. Rising he walked away and returned with one of the square pieces of cloth that she kept for cleaning or covering wounds.

As she took it from his hand, their fingers touched. In that moment something happened, that was so strong that it forced them to pull their hands back. They stared at each other for what seemed an eternity and then she wiped her tears away with the cloth.

"Do ye weep for the child or for yerself?" he asked softly.

"I understand not what ye mean My Lord." she replied.

"I would understand a few tears at this babe's pain, but ye weep, as though, ye weep for a greater loss. Did ye lose a child Emma?" he asked, yet oddly feared her reply.

His question stunned Emma. How did he come to that thought? Did he not know that she was still a maiden?

"Nay My Lord I lost no babe" she replied but her tone was colder than it had ever been before. If he thought it of her, then he looked at her as one with no character. He would not have asked that of a woman he thought of as a lady. But then no lady would have been found being sold, she acknowledged to herself.

Raul noted the coldness in her reply but continued to converse.

"Then ye weep for the child ye will never know, is that yer sorrow?" he continued.

"My Lord, a child was never fated for me. Promised to the Abbey or wed to ye, both options promised me no child." she replied

"Now that we are wed, would ye want a child?" he asked.

"Nay My Lord, for one day ye would hate it for taking away yer dream." she replied.

"I would never hate my child." he cut in.

"Mayhaps not My Lord, but like yer father, ye would then just be disappointed in him." with that, she once again touched the babe.

Raul looked from one to the other. Her hard countenance has softened again. Her gentleness had returned. She even expressed love with those eyes. And all for a stranger!

He wanted to argue that she was wrong. Had he ever had a child, he would have loved it, without conditions. No expectation would be put on it and no duties demanded. He would have been an ideal father.

"Emma, if I had a child of my own…."he tried but was cut short.

"We waste energy on an argument that will never be proven, Ye will be a Templar Knight and a Templar Knight cannot be a father." she cut in again..

He wanted to tell her that he had begun to doubt his commitment to the idea of joining the Order, when she continued

"And it is best it remain that way, for our babe would take away from us, our freedom." she concluded.

That comment brought an end to the conversation and, to the hope.

As the babe, awakened, and the pain made itself felt, she whimpered.  Emma, rose and got some more poppy seed infusion.

"I would that she not sleep now, but the pain will be unbearable if she remains awake. She is so small, that the poppy seed infusion works quickly so I must give very little at a time."

"While she sleeps, why not ye, rest as well. I will keep watch and awaken ye, if she frets." he offered.

"Nay My Lord, I must watch her myself. I will lie here with the babe. It is best ye rest in the keep. I will keep Winifred with me." she suggested.

"Nay, I will rest in the pallet here." was his only answer.

"Yer men await ye at supper." she added.

"I will leave as soon as Winifred comes, but I will not be long. We will have our meal here." he decided for them.

"My Lord, why has the mother not come to see her babe?" she asked.

"She suffers from shock, the physician has been to see her, and says she is much distressed and blames herself."

"But it was an accident, was it not?" she queried.

"She has not been herself since the babe was born." he replied.

"I know many who suffer melancholy after they give birth. I will visit her once the babe is well. If she suffers as the other women, it will be wise her husband does not leave her alone." She said, and Raul offered to talk to Anthony about it.

Soon after, Winifred came and Raul left for the great hall. Winifred had brought an apple for Emma to partake. Emma was most grateful, for her stomach rumbled with hunger.

As she ate her eyelids fluttered. At Winifred's insistence she lay down after seeking a promise that if she fell asleep, Winifred would wake her at the slightest movement from the babe. And then just as promptly as she placed her head down, she fell asleep.

Raul returned to find Winifred watching over the babe and his bride sleeping. Dismissing her he took the seat beside the babe. When he saw the first movement from the babe, he did what he had seen Emma do; he gently patted her good arm. Within moments the babe settled back to sleep again. Raul had fought many battle, defeated many enemies, overcome many obstacles, but none had given him the satisfaction of knowing that he had settle a babe. He then looked at his bride. He understood now why the Order of the Templars demanded chastity and wanted unmarried applicants. How could any man leave his bride and infant babe, and go to war, in foreign lands for unknown periods? He realised now, if he had a babe, it would not leave his sight. The knowledge shook him to his core and weakened the warrior in him.

Another hour passed before Emma's eyes flickered open and she sprung upright.

"The babe is fine. Do not fret Emma, for she sleeps." Raul spoke gently.

"Winifred should have woken me 'ere she left." Emma complained.

"I bid her not to, ye were tired. Ye needed the sleep while the babe sleeps. She will need ye when she wakes." he spoke.

Emma noted Raul's hand gently patting the babe. How odd it was to see a battle hardened warrior display such gentleness.

"I see yer heart is not so hard." she remarked.

"I fight not with my heart but with my head. Battles do not harden my heart." he replied.

"That is good to hear My Lord, for as a Templar knight ye will have much use for a gentle heart." she joked.

Raul smiled before he solemnly replied "When I leave as Templar Knight it is my soul that I shall take with me. My heart! That, I will leave in Kinsborough."

For many moments the two stared at each other. Did she dare ask him what he meant?

Did he dare elaborate on what he had said?

Winifred's arrival with their supper broke their gaze.

Their meal was eaten in silence, both making every attempt at keeping their gaze averted. Both looked at the babe often while Winifred looked at them just as much. When the meal was over and both had not spoken, Winifred breached the silence.

"My Lady, I will secure all at the keep and return to be with ye soon".

"Winifred, stay at the keep. I remain here with yer lady." Raul replied.

The night began with each taking turn to rest while the other cared for the infant. The babe slept peacefully through the night. By morn Anthony and his bride were waiting outside the sick room for permission to enter.

Emma took one look at the mother and realised that she has fretted for naught, for the mother loved her babe and would not intentionally harm it. If she only suffered from melancholy then Emma had herbs that could help.

"I can see where yer thought ventures My Lady." Raul whispered.

"It remains well and truly in this room, My Lord." she replied.

"One sick room is not enough, ye seek now to become a physician!" he remarked.

"What harm is there in that My Lord? I could care for the women and children, and the physician could look to the men" she replied.

"Ye are the lady of Kinsborough, ye have other duties as well." he reminded.

"Nay My Lord, Winifred, can look to the keep, she knows it well. While ye fight with swords, the enemy without, we will fight with herbs, the enemy within." she replied

"And when, My Lady, did ye think of this?" he queried.

"At night as I watched the babe and ye sleep and knew neither would need me in just a few days. Ye, My Lord, will join the crusades and this babe will heal and return to her parent's care. If my future is at Kinsborough then I must be of use."

"Ye have already done much for Kinsborough." Raul began.

"Nay My Lord, it is but the beginning." she replied

"My Lady plans much without me." While Raul was pleased that Emma had begun to think of Kinsborough as her permanent home, it irked him that she was planning much for Kinsborough and seemed to forget that he was the Baron.

"Its best ye get accustomed to it, My Lord, for ye will be away many months and will not be here to voice yer thoughts. I too unhappily prepare myself to take decisions on my own for Kinsborough and her people, for My Lord leaves much responsibility on me." she commented.

While everything Emma uttered was the truth, it was bitter and unpalatable and gave Raul much to think about. When it irked him that Emma would be deciding all for Kinsborough, then how would he ever be able to leave the castle to a stranger to inherit?

He also understood his father's need to secure a line of succession. Whatever Raul felt about his life at Wilbert, it did not alter that fact that Wilbert was a family seat and must always remain so. The pressure that he had hoped to remove from himself, of producing the next heir now returned and seated itself firmly upon his shoulder.

He looked at Emma. He had life exactly as he had planned it, but suddenly it appeared all wrong. The only picture that seemed right was of him sharing Kinsborough with Emma and their kids. A picture that he himself had ensured would never come true.

He recalled what Peter had earlier told him "Before ye follow through with ye plan, think this Raul, yer plan does not account for the human heart".

He had been especially pleased with his choice of bride for she had felt just as him. She too had wanted to be unbound and free. And it was that very desire that had now begun to vex him.

It bothered him went he saw her busy herself in the sick room, it irritated him when she thought a sick person was more interesting than him. It annoyed him when she did not join him for their nightly stroll, because some child had decided that they would only sleep if Emma rested with them. But most of all it made him wild when she beamed with happiness at the sight of a wild herb plant that she found and then run off with the physician to test the plant out. It mattered not that the physician was old enough to be her grandfather. It only mattered that she always put someone or something ahead of him. Again and again he would remember Peter's words 'What if either of ye want differently after ye both are wed?"

Chapter 19

Raul had gone on patrol duty with several of his knights. Emma had tended to the two men in the sick room and was on her way to the keep when the guards announced the arrival of a riding party. With Raul away, Sir Rowan was approached for permission to permits them into the castle.

Rowan was just steps away from Emma which made it impossible for Emma not to hear the name of the person at the gate. Rosalie! She tried desperately not to show any emotions on her face, but try as she might she was unable to ignore the curiosity that had arisen in her. What did Rosalie look like? Why was she here? Had Raul invited her? Had Raul been meeting her even though he was wed?

Rowan too was in a quandary. Standing beside him was the Lady of Kinsborough and standing outside the gate was the woman his lord had once loved. How could he insult the former by opening the gates to the latter? Peter was better at handling situations like this, but it had been his turn to go with Raul.

"Sir Rowan, ye keep my lord's guest waiting? He will be displeased." she said with a smile.

"My Lord, spoke not of Rosalie's arrival. I have no permission to let her in, My Lady." he replied.

"Rosalie must have a reason to visit and ye have my permission to allow her in." she answered.

"But My Lady, Rosalie is, ..."he got no further.

"Is a woman who has travelled far and is in need of rest. Kinsborough welcomed me, a stranger to yer lord, surely it is more right that Kinsborough welcome one, who is already his friend." she replied as serenely as possible.

"As My Lady wishes" Sir Rowan replied, glad the decision had been taken for him though he remained unsure if the decision was the right one.

His permission was shouted up to the guards and the drawbridge was lowered. As the gate rose, Winifred came rushing to Emma's side.

"My Lady what folly, do ye do now? Ye permit the woman who could take yer future from ye by entering yer present." she whispered.

"Winifred, Rosalie had the Baron's past, I had his present, the Order of the Templar, has his future. What fear I, when his future is already lost to the third?"

"My Lady, until ye opened that gate, my lord's future was in yer hands. Now ye bring in stronger winds outside yer control. It will change even that which is ordained." Winifred expressed her fear.

"Do not fear that wind Winifred. If I left that gate shut, would that wind not have entered over the walls. And if I shut every window in the castle, would I be able to survive without the air, I seal out?".

Winifred looked at Emma. Despite the brave words, she saw the worry in Emma's face. Her lady was not as unaffected as she pretended. She saw the same look that she had seen many moons ago, on the face of her mistress. It was the night Maja had entered Wilbert, under the pretext of having lost her way. Now another woman was entering a castle with the power to hurt its lady. And Winifred, as wise and prophetic as she was, remained as helpless to stop it happen.

Emma in the meanwhile kept her eyes focused on the gate. She was not surprised when she saw a beautiful woman ride in escorted by two knights. What did surprise her was that both knights carried the insignia of Wilbert on their flag.

As Rosalie reached the center of the bailey, she was aided by one of the knights to dismount. Slowly, as though with tired limbs she walked towards Emma and reaching her curtsied. While Rosalie's beauty had not surprised Emma, Emma's looks had astonished Rosalie. Emma had been described as a pale woman with no beauty, yet the woman who stood in front of her, had a glow and warmth that she had not seen in many. And when she had smiled, she displayed an uncommon beauty. Why then had Maja lied to her?

"My Lady, I express my gratitude at being permitted to enter." Rosalie spoke in soft voice.

"Kinsborough welcomes ye Rosalie. My Lord is away but ye are welcome to stay." Emma welcomed her.

Emma then asked Winifred to organise refreshment in the great hall for the three visitors.

"Thank ye My Lady, I see ye are surprised by my visit. I understood Baron Kinsborough knew of it." Rosalie said

That comment worried Emma. If Raul knew Rosalie was coming, why had he not mentioned anything to her and why had he gone away on patrol duty and left her to face this situation?

"It matters not. The Baron will be glad that ye arrived safely. Come, ye can rest in the great hall while we wait for yer refreshments." she invited.

Just as they turned towards the keep, the sound of the lowering of the drawbridge was heard again. Since no permission was asked of Sir Rowan, it meant only one thing. Baron Raul was entering himself.

All stood frozen in their places. Emma watched Rosalie's face, Sir Rowan watched Emma's and Winifred looked towards Raul as he entered.

Riding towards his castle, all Raul had thought about was seeing Emma again. He had left halfheartedly and he had returned with eagerness. Now as he approached Emma he sensed that something was amiss. Seeing Emma standing at the base of the steps as if to welcome him had been a joy to behold, until he realised that she had not once looked at him. Instead Emma was looking at the woman beside her. Curious, he turned to look at that woman and pulled the reigns so suddenly that Daktonian, rose on his hind leg. Rosalie? What was she doing at Kinsborough and with Emma?

"My Lord" Rosalie curtsied, but when she looked up, the Baron was again looking at his lady.

Emma curtsied to him and greeted Sir Peter, and then turned to walk up the steps.

"My Lady, wait." Raul voice came across.

Emma halted a second and then turned to face Raul.

"Ye will remain." he commanded.

"My Lord, I am needed in the sick room. I must return there." she replied.

Raul knew Emma was using the sick room as an excuse. He also knew that forcing her to stay, would not go down well. He had hoped she had comprehended his meaning. That she had understood that he wished her to remain with him when he conversed with Rosalie.

"In that case Sir Peter and Winifred will remain with ye." was all he ended up saying

"My Lord, Sir Peter must be in need of rest. I am able to look after myself." Emma countered.

Raul looked at his friend. That look was enough

'My Lady, it will be a pleasure." With that he dismounted and followed Emma towards the sick room

"Ye should defy yer lord sometimes; it would do ye good." She expressed in anger.

"Aye My Lady, just as it has done ye good." Sir Peter replied with a smile.

Before Raul led Rosalie away to the great hall, he turned to Rowan

"See that the men with Rosalie are disarmed. They carry my father's flag, but they are Maja's men. What made ye permit Rosalie to enter?" he questioned.

"I did not My Lord, our lady gave the command upon hearing Rosalie's name." Rowan cleared.

"Command the guard that no one is to leave the castle especially not with my bride." Raul directed

'Ye suspect treachery?" Rowan asked.

"I find it strange that Maja leaves and Rosalie arrives." Raul replied.

All the while Rosalie watched Raul. Maja had said that the Baron still loved her, but he seemed more concerned with conversing with Sir Peter and Sir Rowan than with seeing her.

She wondered if he too felt a stranger as she did. The man who stood in front of her was just as handsome as the lad she had known, but the man was no longer taken by her beauty as the lad had been.  It was almost as if he had never known her.

"Come Rosalie, we will talk in the great hall. I have asked Sir Rowan to join us when he is done"

He does not even want to be alone with me, that is not a sign of a man in love, Rosalie thought. Was Maja mistaken? Maja had spoken of a loveless marriage betwixt the Baron and his lady. Maja had assured her that the Baron still pined for her. And she had promised that even Lord Wilbert would rather see Rosalie in Raul's life that his wedded lady.

So far nothing had made sense. The lady was not as plain as Maja had made her out to be. The Baron had not even noticed her, despite her standing right in front of him, all the while looking at his bride. Even now he did not wish to be alone with her. First he had willed his bride to be present and now Sir Rowan. Something was amiss.

As they entered the great hall, a maid brought a pitcher filled with mead. This they had as they sat at the table.

"My Lord, I understood, ye expected my arrival." Rosalie remarked.

"Who gave ye to understand that?" He queried.

"Lady Wilbert. She sent word ahead of our party. The men left two nights prior. Did they not come here?" she queried.

"No one came and no message arrived, but then that is the usual case with the new lady of Wilbert." Raul replied and then continued "Why come now Rosalie? Ye are wedded are ye not?"

"I was My Lord, I have since been widowed." she replied.

The knowledge that Rosalie was now free did nothing to change his heartbeat. Oddly he found it vexing that his ordered life was being inconvenienced.

"How long have ye been thus?" he asked

"Twelve moons My Lord." she answered

"Why did ye not come earlier when I was unwed, why come now, when I have a bride?" he asked again

"Because I was told that ye wed to seek revenge on Lord Bruce, because we had been parted. That ye still wished me in yer life and that ye wished to be free of yer vows." she decided to be honest.

"And all this, the new Lady of Wilbert said to ye?" when Rosalie nodded he continued "And the new Lady of Wilbert did not offer ye more coins to come?"

How did he know that Maja had offered her exactly that? If he knew that, then did he know that she had refused it this time?

"I know she also offered ye land before. Ye accepted that land in place of me. I would be right would I not, in saying, that she has paid ye handsomely to try and take now, what ye left behind before - a husband!" Raul found that he was not bitter about the trade. In some ways it eased the guilt he had always felt since knowing that Rosalie had been married off because of him.

"Ra..My Lord. I had no option then. I was a mason's daughter. Lord Wilbert would never have let us wed. That land gave my father a home to call his own. My marriage to a soldier gave me respectability. It is more than what ye would have been allowed to give." She explained.

Raul was silent. He had always believed that Rosalie had been married off against her wishes. It was from Sir Maximillian that he learnt of late, of the money and the land that had exchanged hands between Maja and Rosalie. But it was not Rosalie's actions that had disturbed him. It was Maja's. What was she gaining by pushing Rosalie back into his life now after deliberately separating them before? Be it Emma or Rosalie, Maja's niece would still not be wed to him, so why bring Rosalie back into his life?

"Rosalie, ye have been misinformed. I am a wedded man now and I take my vows seriously. I will not break my vows either for the past or for the future." he clarified ensuring that she understood that he had a new life now and one that no longer included their past.

Rosalie was silent for some moments and then she said "My Lord, I would not have that sin on my soul."

"If that be yer honest answer then, Kinsborough welcomes ye Rosalie," Then seeing Rowan enter, he rose saying "I will leave ye in Sir Rowan's care while I seek out my bride."

From Rowan's expression it was obvious that he had heard the last of the conversation so Raul did not have to explain how matters stood.

"Sir Rowan, Rosalie and her party will stay tonight. Ask Winifred to look to their needs." Raul moved to leave the room with this final instruction.

Rowan nodded, then whispered "It would be wise that ye break yer vow My Lord, for the people of Kinsborough want only our lady Emma in yer life, as ye true bride."

Raul smiled "Since I cannot break my vow, I must see to it, that she breaks hers."

Raul had just reached the doorway when Rosalie halted him. From her next words, he knew she had heard some of his whispered comment.

"My Lord! Ye said earlier that ye took yer marriage vows seriously. If that be right then do not tarry too long in making yer marriage true. The lady of Wilbert seeks an annulment even as we speak." Rosalie warned.

"On, what grounds?" Raul asked,

"A virgin marriage, My Lord" she replied.

"The new Lady of Wilbert continues to underestimate my will and tests my patience. Let her try", Then he was gone.

"Sir Rowan, I fear, it is the Baron who underestimates Lady Maja. The people of Wilbert have long believed that the first Lady of Wilbert did not fall by accident, ye see, Lady Maja was seen coming down the steps soon after the fall, yet she declared that she was not at Wilbert when it happened."

"Why has no one told Baron Raul about it, if that be true?" Sir Rowan asked.

"Because, the woman who saw Lady Maja, soon after disappeared and took the secret with her. Without that woman, there was no witness to speak up." Rosalie said.

"And who was that woman?" Sir Rowan asked.

"My mother, Sir Rowan." she replied.

Rowan knew two things from the moment the words had been uttered. The first that Rosalie could not return to Wilbert until the mystery had been solved. And since it was not wise for her to stay at Kinsborough, it meant that he would have to send her to his manor as Peter's was barred to women. The second was that Raul must be told of this find. And it must be done soon. For if the first lady of Wilbert had been murdered, then, not only were Lord Bruce and Baron Raul in mortal danger but it also meant that Lady Kinsborough would be her next target.

Raul walked over to the sick room but did not find Emma there. He next went to Emma's room and again it was empty. Finally noticing that the door to his old room was ajar, he looked in.

His bed was back there and his garments hung on the peg. And both Winifred and Emma were seeing to the bath being placed back in the room.

"What is the meaning of this, My Lady?" he questioned though kept his voice even. He saw Emma look uncomfortable before replying.

"I believe ye will sleep better here My Lord."

"Ah but I slept best, in the other room My Lady." he replied. The squires having settled the bath, left the room pretending they had not heard anything. Winifred too began to move towards the door saying that she would go to the next room and prepare it for Rosalie.

"Rosalie will sleep below with the other women." Lord Raul replied.

"That will not be proper My Lord. The room beside yers is being prepared." Emma spoke up.

"Why next door?" he questioned.

"Because these rooms share a parapet" She replied. Surely Raul would know that she was making it easy for him to meet Rosalie without the household becoming aware of it.

"I am a wedded man Emma, place another woman in yer place, and ye make her my whore." he replied ensuring that he maintained that even key.

"I do not call her that, My Lord" she spoke again.

"The whole castle will call her that, if ye continue with yer plan" Raul replied.

"Nay My Lord, it is I, who will be worthy of that title" she replied.

"Ye are my wedded bride. It is a fact ye have chosen to forget on many occasions. It is one that I have not forgotten yet." he commented.

"Then it is best ye do so now, My Lord. I have long heard of the great love ye had for Rosalie. I have witnessed the anger ye still hold against yer father on being separated." she explained but found that Raul had cut in.

"My anger with my father is more to do with his treatment of my mother and his marriage to Maja, than with Rosalie and me." he replied.

"Did ye not choose a bride, who would have less breeding than Rosalie, to vex yer father? Did ye not choose a monastic life for ye did not want to give yer heart to another? Deny these My Lord and I will change my plan." she challenged.

"I cannot deny it My Lady, for there is truth in what ye have said, but often times, life gives what it thinks best for us. It is best to accept what destiny is offering us." he whispered

"My Lord, I wish for an honest reply to my query. If ye could turn time, and go back to yer youth, would ye have wedded Rosalie?" she questioned.

Raul thought about her question. He probably would have married Rosalie but it would have been for more wrong reasons than right ones. But if there was one thing he was sure of now, it was that he had never truly loved Rosalie. If he loved any woman in his life, it was Emma. Yet even wedded to her he was unable to tell her of it.

"Do not answer it My Lord, for I have my reply." she spoke

"I would give my answer anyway. Rosalie and I may have wed, but ..." he began

"Ye still can My Lord." she cut in.

"Ye make a habit to forget that I am a wedded man." he remarked.

"Nay My Lord, ye were never a wedded man." she returned.

"What jest is this Emma?" he questioned with irritation.

"My Lord, I am not of Rosemund, and nor is my name Emma" she replied.

"Again I ask what jest is this Emma?" he growled this time.

"My Lord, the woman ye wed in the chapel was named Emma, but that is not my true name. Our wedding vows are not valid. There is no longer a need to annul our marriage. For, it exists not. In the eyes of the law, My Lord, I am not yer bride."

Raul took many moments to ingest this information. Then walking over to his chest he removed their wedding scroll, and there on the parchment, he saw their signatures. His stated clearly, Baron Raul of Kinsborough. Hers only had one name, Emma.

"So ye lied to yer God and ye lied to me! With what intent?" He questioned trying to remain calm.

"I believe I did not lie My Lord. If I am guilty of anything it is that I withheld the truth" she tried to hold on to her composure.

"My Lady, withholding the truth, is lying. It is but disguised. The line between them is very slim". His deep voice had become louder.

"Yet there remains that line, My Lord. And I choose to believe that I withheld the truth." she answered.

"What is yer real name then?" he asked

"I cannot say My Lord. It will endanger the lives of many including ye".

"A warrior takes that risk when he chooses his profession. A knight embraces danger. I am willing to take that risk" he replied,

"Mayhaps, but I am not, My Lord." she replied.

"Why reveal this truth now?" he asked

"Ye have a lady in yer castle, who ye once wished to wed. She is free of her commitment. Ye My Lord, must not be bound by yers." was her response.

"And where do ye place yerself in yer plan for my future?".

"Where I always was My Lord, an indebted visitor in yer life." she replied.

"Ye have lived as a bride in my castle and in the eyes of people, ye have shared my room, if ye tell the world of this truth, do ye know what ye will be called?" he asked.

She had thought deeply of this before she had decided to walk away from his life.

"My Lord, where I go, it matters not what I am called. Only the people of Kinsborough will know of this secret." were the words she uttered.

"Ye forget, so will the people of Wilbert, our travelling Friar, and the sick who came for cure. There are many that will carry the tale." he said hoping his words would worry her.

"And with not one of them, would I be crossing paths with, in the future. My Lord, ye married me knowing me to be a kitchen maid. Knowing that, it did not tarnish me in the eyes of yer people. Pray cease yer worry for my good name. Believe me, My Lord it is of no import." she pleaded.

"That is because we were wed. Emma hear me on this, it matters not what yer true name is, I would that we remain wed."

"My Lord, our wedded life may not be real, but it would be intolerable for me to live in the same keep as yer other woman." Emma expressed her fear.

"What other woman?" he questioned.

"Rosalie My Lord! How can ye forget, she is the reason for this conversation." she remarked with frustration.

"Emma, I hope ye understand I need to call ye by a name and Emma is the only one I have unless ye choose to give me another." he asked.

"Tis best ye only know me as Emma, My Lord" she replied refusing to divulge further.

"Are ye already wed Emma?" Raul asked this question fearing the answer. For the first time his inner self trembled with the fear of the dreaded reply.

"Nay My Lord, I am not wed." she replied

"Ah, ye lie, for ye forget we wed not long ago" he remarked.

"No My Lord, I forget nothing, for neither was our wedding real, nor our marriage."

"That My Lady can be corrected." As he made a move towards her and she in turn made a move toward the parapet he froze, as the image of her swaying on it appeared before his eyes. It was too big a risk to take.

"Ye say ye were not wed, were ye betrothed?" he asked trying to take her attension away and when his question was met with silence, the knife of jealousy pierced his heart and he knew what true pain was. The thought of her wanting to belong to another, destroyed his composure.

"Why did ye not wed him then?" he growled

"Because My Lord, it was not for me." she replied unnerved by his anger.

"Was the betrothal not of yer choosing then?" he asked.

"Nay My Lord, neither the betrothal nor the betrothed." she replied.

"On the day we met, ye said, ye were going to the Abbey on yer father's command, did ye imply that ye do not choose the veil either?" he asked the crucial question.

"Nay My Lord, if that is what my father wished by commanding me to go there, then that life too was chosen for me." she replied.

"What then is of yer choosing" he queried

Emma smiled. She wondered what Raul would do if she said, that the only thing she would like to choose would be Raul for a husband and Kinsborough as her home. But she could never ask that. Not when she knew Rosalie was now free.

"My Lord, it would be, to see ye wed to the woman of yer choosing." she replied.

"So be it, Emma, if that is what ye truly wish." he said in a lowered voice.

"It is My Lord" she said, and with it her heart shattered into a hundred pieces.

"Then I invite ye to my wedding Emma, for I wed again tonight." he announced and with that, Raul walked out of the room and asked the guard to fetch the Friar. And without saying another word or even looking back, he walked down the stairwell. No one saw his smile.

After he had left, Emma sat on the edge of the bed. She had done what was right, so why did her heart feel as if things were so very wrong.

The news of a second marriage, so soon after the first, created havoc in the castle. When the news reached Peter and Rowan, they both rushed to Raul's side.

"Raul pray, tell us, what game do ye play now. Ye are already wed." Peter spoke first.

"So I believed, but My Lady tells me that our wedding was not a legal one, for she is not Emma of Rosemund"

"We have been aware of that since yer father's illness. Why does that change the situation now?" Rowan interjected.

"It appears she is not from Rosemund as we already knew, but she is not even 'Emma'. She chooses to hide her real name but as she signed her name as Emma on the parchment, our wedding is not lawful either" Raul explained.

"So what do ye plan now?" Rowan asked.

"I will wed again" he replied.

"Raul, what matter what her name was or is, for the people of Kinsborough she is our lady. Or is it that ye wish to wed another?" Peter questioned

"Does Rosalie know that ye are now free to wed her?" Rowan asked.

"Peter ye rightly said, it matters not what her name was or is. In the eyes of my God, I have accepted her as my bride, I will not choose another. Emma will remain my bride. But I need, wed her again. The Law demands a name she is known by to make it lawful." he replied.

"If ye know not her true name, what name will ye create to make it lawful?" Peter asked

Raul smiled. "The only name we all know Emma by, 'Lady Emma of Kinsborough'. Friar Joseph requests five witnesses to certify at the altar that they know my bride as Lady Emma of Kinsborough."

"Raul ye waste yer time, desiring to be a Templar Knight, politics and intrigue are yer strength." Sir Peter remarked his voice ringing with amusement.

Raul stalled for a moment. Not only had the desire to be a Templar Knight vanished, he had even forgotten that such had been his aim. Guilt rose for a moment.

"Raul, I always knew destiny chose a different path for ye. Ye serve England that is enough, be it as a Templar Knight or as a Warrior Lord. The sire needs sword arms and coins. I will provide him the arm, ye my friend, can provide him with the coin. So we would still battle together"

Peter's words made sense. Everything that had happened in his life had happened for a reason or caused a reaction. Had his mother not died, he would not have been sent away to become the mighty warrior he had become. Had he married Rosalie, what would he have done when Emma came into his life? And their meeting was fated, that he knew.

"And what of Lady Emma, does she walk to the altar, willingly again?" Rowan asked

"Yes my bride, will still come willingly but she thinks she comes to wed me to another." Raul laughed, and then looking at Peter he added "Yes ye can ask her again once she is there, I can see ye still wish to remain her defender."

As the sun, lowered over the castle wall, the skyline was broken with the dust that rose, as three riders, neared the castle. Richard the Lionheart's insignia caused an immediate lowering of the drawbridge.

Raul, Peter and Rowan rushed to meet their sire only to find that the King had sent an urgent missive. He wanted Raul to meet him not two hours ride from them. At first Raul thought it was a ruse, but the king's seal took away any doubts.

With the sire so near, Raul delegated Rowan with the care of the castle and with Peter and other knights, prepared to leave.

He was disappointed that Emma did not come to bid them farewell. Rosalie stood beside Rowan. It was as he turned Daktonian towards the gate that Rosalie stepped forward and said 'My Lord, I bid ye goodbye. I leave tomorrow and the kings bidding can keep ye away long. I beseech ye My Lord, do not underestimate, Lady Wilbert. She would have Lady Kinsborough gone."

Raul looked at Rosalie a moment before replying "I thank ye Rosalie. I regret things could not be different betwixt us. Ye are welcome to stay longer and Sir Rowan can see ye home when I return" Then turning to Rowan he added, "See that My Lady is always in yer sight. I charge ye, and Winifred to keep My Lady safe."

With that Raul bowed to Rosalie and clasped the palm of Rowan. And then he chanced to look up. There on the wall walk, stood Emma. As they eyes met, he bowed and she returned the courtesy but did not attempt to move. He had hoped on seeing him she would come to see him off but her immovable stance dashed that hope. The next minute he placed his spangenhelm on his head, turned and joining the others rode through the gate.

Emma looked at the scene before her. The last time Raul had ridden away, she had stood down in the bailey and forced him to take her with him. This time he rode away, that right had been taken from her, and the woman who would soon be his bride, had taken on that privilege.

To say that she was pained at the knowledge that he had not come to bid goodbye would understate what she felt. She had not even been told why he rode and for how long he would be gone?

Chapter 20

Raul and Peter rode hard, followed closely by the knights until two hours later, they neared Manor Dover. It shared the same direction to where he had found Emma. Was it coincidence that the king called him to the same area? Was his king upset that he had wed without permission? But the king was away at a secret location and waiting had not been an option. Or had the king called him to see him prisoner for bidding on the sale of a woman? Why else had the king not come to Kinsborough and instead asked him to come here.

That fear however dissolved as he entered the great hall and King Richard smiled at their approach. They both approached their sire and knelt before him in respect.

"Baron Raul, Sir Peter, I knew I could depend on ye both. Come we to need talk at once"

"Lords and Gentlemen, I introduce ye all to Baron Raul and Sir Peter. Baron Raul's castle is two hours from here, and both are familiar with this region. I chose not to ride there, for our trail ended here and it is best we continue the search from this place."

The King then asked everyone to introduce themselves. Before the last warrior introduced himself, the king spoke again.

"This here is Lord Andrew of Roseborough. He and his sister are my wards. Lord Andrew was wounded in battle and was rumoured dead. I appointed a guardian to care for Clarissa who is his older by two years. Andrew by the Grace of our Lord, had not died but was found in the battlefield and nursed by the Hospitallers. He returned a few moons ago, to find his sister gone. The guardian I appointed died soon after and another had appointed himself in that place. We learnt Sir Drake had betrothed himself to Clarissa in a bid to claim Roseborough."

"And why do ye believe Lady Clarissa to be here Sire?" Raul asked knowing in his heart that he was taking his bride's name.

"Clarissa was journeying to the Abbey of St.Mary when the party was attacked. The servant who travelled with her was wounded and survived by some miracle. Clarissa was captured by the attackers. The incident happened but a two hours ride from here"

The hairs on his nape stood on end. He did not need to know the rest of what had happened, for he was part of all that had occurred after.

"We began our search from where the party was attacked. The servant saw Clarissa being taken away but was unable to rescue her. We have learnt that three women were sold soon after. We traced the first two but neither of them was Lady Clarissa. Lord Andrew has heard that the third left with a knight in the direction of Kinsborough. It is why we seek yer help. Ye know this area well and ye know the knights. My ward must be found"

Raul and Peter exchanged glances.

"What share ye both?" the king asked noting the look they exchanged.

"Sire, if I be permitted, may I inquire a few particulars from Lord Andrew" Raul asked.

"Baron Raul, is there something ye know?" Andrew spoke for the first time.

"Lord Andrew, I do not know if we speak of the same lady. When say ye, this happened?" Raul asked,

"Four moons prior, My Lord" Andrew spoke and all heard the hope in his voice.

"Does Lady Clarissa have hazel eyes and hair the colour of walnut, My Lord?"

Lord Andrew reached out to grip Raul's arm "Pray tell me, she is alive!" he pleaded.

'Sire, if Lord Andrew and I speak of the same lady, then she is alive, but the lady I speak of goes by another name." Raul addressed the king.

"Would that name be Emma?" Andrew's voice was a prayer now.

Raul jerked his head towards Andrew and then looked at Peter. How was he ever going to explain to their sire, of how he had come to wed the king's ward? He understood now why she kept her name hidden. She was a royal ward, and betrothed to her guardian.

"Aye My Lord, my bride, goes by the name of Emma." Raul declared.

A hush fell over the crowd and Andrew's grip tightened further.

"Ye are wed to Lady Clarissa?" said the king breaking the silence

"Aye sire. She was being sold by her attackers. The only way for me to rescue her was to bid for her. She wanted to go to the Abbey and travelled with me to Kinsborough. I needed a bride sire, and she, a place where she would be safe. Our marriage was of mutual agreement. She said nothing of her past save that her father was steward to the Lord of Rosemund."

The king laughed. "Steward she called her father, did she? Raul, her father was not only Lord of Roseborough, but he was also my secret advisor who went by the name of " The Fox".  I named him Lord of Rosemund when he went on missions to the Holy Land for me. Andrew and Clarissa accompanied him on the shorter ones and she would spend her time with the physician learning about the herbs and helping him to heal. It is that love of hers that caused me to christen her Emma, 'Healer of the Universe'."

"She said not one of these" Raul admitted, disappointed that Emma had not trusted him enough to confide in him but gladdened to hear the last sentence.  He noted that Peter smiled too. It meant that he too had understood the importance of what had been said.

"Is she happy, Baron Raul?" Andrew asked after seeking permission to once again address Raul.

"Lord Andrew, it is best ye judge for yerself. My reply might be tainted with wishes. Ye are all welcome to come and meet Lady Emma of Kinsborough." Raul responded.

The king rose, and immediately announced that they would depart for Kinsborough.

Two hours seemed longer as they journeyed back. If Emma had known how many, eagerly awaited to be with her, she would have been filled with joy. This thought also brought with it the fear that she would now leave, for they were no longer bound by matrimony unless he could make her accept the vows they had pledged.

Finally the high walls of Kingsborough came into view. It impressed all as it was intended to. The king had been there before, but much had changed and had been improved.

The gates stood open in anticipation. His guards looked composed and the people came out in numbers to greet their lord and their much loved Sire.

As soon as Raul had stepped into the bailey he sensed something amiss. He looked around but could not see Rowan or Emma. Even if Emma had not come down, Rowan would never make that error of not formally welcoming their King, for it was akin to treason.

Winifred stood there with his squire but he could not see the others.

After Winifred extended her courtesy to their Sire, she looked at Raul in puzzlement.

"My Lord, I see not My Lady" Winifred asked.

"Yer lady should be with ye or in the castle" he replied, though that niggling worry grew by the moment.

"My Lord, ye jest, for they rode to ye." she replied.

"Who and when?" his voice had risen, drawing everyone's attension. His first thought was 'Oh God, she has left."

"An hour ago My Lord, our sire's messenger came with a missive for our lady to follow ye. Sir Rowan, and ..." Winifred spoke

"I sent no messenger!" the king barked.

"Sire, the missive lies in the great hall" Winifred replied taken aback by the tone and the implication of the words.

"Bring it forthwith" The king ordered and Raul immediately asked his squire to fetch it.

Hearing the order, his squire ran toward the hall and was back within moments with the missive in hand.

Bowing, he handed it to the King. The king looked at the note, then at the seal behind. Then he handed it to Raul. Someone had used his seal to endorse a false document, for the missive was not sent by him. This was treason and by heaven that person would welcome death.

Raul and Andrew read the missive with growing apprehension. The king in the missive had demanded his ward return immediately.

"Lord Andrew, whoever wrote this, was known to ye house, for he speaks of a ward. And none here knew of that status. What happened to her guardian?" he asked.

"We do not know. When I returned to Roseborough he was gone, I feared he had taken Clarissa, on hearing that he had betrothed himself to her, using another missive with our Sire's seal. But I learnt that she had run away with my father's servant and no other. Lord help him, when I see that man" Andrew replied with anger clearly marking his countenance.

"Lord Andrew, ye will not strike the blow. Sir Drake has committed treason. His punishment lies at my hand." the King counseled.

"Sire ye ask a difficult thing when I have failed my sister once already." Andrew replied.

"What say ye Baron Raul? Do ye want the privilege of executing Sir Drake as well?" the King asked.

"No sire, but if my bride is harmed, I will witness it." Raul spoke words that he would never have dared before. His obedience had always been unquestionable.

"I see marriage has not been all good, for ye, challenge yer Sire. We will talk of this later. At this moment my ward's life lies at risk and I see a brother and a husband, equally pained at the loss. Ride then all three of ye and save her. I will follow with my knights as soon as I have eaten.".

Not waiting for another second, Raul, Peter, Andrew and a dozen knights turned to ride out, their swords thirsty for one man's blood.

Suddenly Raul stopped and addressed Winifred

"How many knights rode with My Lady?" Raul asked

"Sir Rowan and five knights, Rosalie also rides with them, My Lord."

Why did Rosalie travel with them he wondered? Then, pushing aside any more questions, he rode out of his gate, not one of the riders had even taken a drop of water since their return.

The king looked at the squire and ordered "Bring us some refreshment at once. We follow them soon."

Chapter 21

From the time they had ridden out of Kinsborough, Rowan sat on edge, his sword and that of the other knights, kept in readiness. He had seen the King's seal, yet he sensed all was not right. The direction they were taking, moved away from that of Raul and Peter. If the King was with Raul and Peter why were they moving in another direction?

He noted that both Lady Emma and Rosalie were equally nervous. He had let Lady Emma persuade him to leave on receiving the message but now he berated his judgement. It would have been better to anger the king than let down his lord.

He really should not have heeded Lady Emma's pleading. Now he needed time to judge the situation and so asked Rosalie to pretend that she needed to make a convenience stop. This done he ensured that the stop was prolonged as much as possible.

From the corner of his eyes he saw a flash of red race past. He lifted his sword. It was a signal to his knights that danger approached.

A second flash confirmed his fears.

"My Lady, all is not right here. If there is an attack, I beseech ye to ride back towards Kinsborough. We will hold them until help arrives." He whispered.

"What help do ye expect, Sir Rowan?" Emma asked.

"The help, that My Lady will send back when she reaches Kinsborough" he smiled with false bravado. The message being clear, that if she did not make it back, no help would be forthcoming. Many lives would depend on her.

With a signal to his knights, they silently attacked the two riders that led them. Tying them up, they turned to return on the path taken but within seconds, mercenaries dressed in black garment and red capes blocked their path. Others dressed in the same garments soon surrounded them from the other three sides.

"Sir Rowan, do not be brave, and get yerself killed." Lady Emma whispered.

"Does My Lady, prefer my death at the hands of her lord?" he smiled with his reply.

"Ye will follow us" The man who appeared the leader, broke into their conversation.

"Who is it that speaks?" Lord Rowan asked.

"It is of no concern to ye. Alight from ye steeds." he ordered.

As Emma moved to follow his order, he sneered "Oh no My Lady, ye will come with us. Yer betrothed eagerly awaits his bride."

Emma had all her questions answered at once. But how had her guardian known where to find her?

"His fight is with me, let everyone else go." she commanded

"My Lady, takes me for a fool. My Lady would do well to remember, that it was me that traced ye to the castle of Kinsborough." he remarked.

"How did ye?" she asked

"No one outbids me My Lady. I knew ye went with Lord Raul of Kinsborough after the sale, and when my friends turned up dead I knew ye remained with him. Had yer betrothed not paid me well for yer return, I would keep ye for myself, as revenge." He sniggered again

"By using the King's seal, ye commit treason, are ye aware of that?" she asked hoping the questions would delay their moves.

"King Richard, is more interested in the crusade, ye know that My Lady. Many have his seal to act in proxy, it matters not if the King thinks it treason, he is not here to act on it, is he?" he sniggered again

"How came ye by the seal then?" she asked.

"My Lady gives me much credit, the seal belongs to yer betrothed. With one stamp he became yer betrothed with another he ordered ye out of Kinsborough." he continued.

"Keep yer mouth closed, Pounder, I sent ye to fetch my betrothed not give them an explanation of how it was done." The voice that uttered the words was known to her.

How often had she been screamed at by that voice, how often had she been threatened?

And she was back where she started. In his clutches!

"Lady Clarissa, ye shock me with yer impertinence. Come, greet yer guardian and yer betrothed." he mocked Emma.

Rowan looked at Lady Emma at the mention of the name Clarissa.

"Lady Clarissa?" he queried with surprise.

"Did she not introduce herself before? Let me undo that neglect. Sir Rowan, that is yer name, is it not?" Drake asked

"Aye" Rowan replied

"Aye Sir! Remember yer place knight." he growled.

When Rowan had not repeated the words, Sir Drake moved toward him. Knowing him capable of heinous acts and depraved cruelty, Emma moved forward.

"Let them go, or I will not return with ye." she spoke up

"Lady Clarissa, ye are in no position to make a bargain. I see being away from Roseborough has loosened yer tongue. It must be remedied for I cannot abide, a woman that knows not her place." With that he rode up to Emma and struck her cheek with the back of his hand. The impact was so strong that it almost dislodged her from her seat.

At this Rowan and his knights raised their swords. Emma saw what a fight now would do. Strategy was one thing that she had learnt from Raul. He had bid on her instead of fighting when it was the path to take, and he fought instead of surrendering when the time was right.

"I am no longer yer ward, Sir Drake. Ye have just struck a wedded woman." she prodded

That news shook Sir Drake. How is it that he had not heard of it?

"Ye lie." he screamed at her

"Would the Lady of Kinsborough lie?" she provoked his anger further.

"Ye surprise me again Lady Clarissa, I feared ye would claim Sir Rowan as yer wedded husband." mocking her he moved toward Rowan

"Sir Rowan is mine." Rosalie spoke up. Sir Drake looked from one to the other and then he burst out laughing.

"I see what ye do. It is a ploy to delay our journey. It is time we leave, come Lady Clarissa, unless ye want to enjoy their screams." He relayed his message with the threat.

Emma had to make her move now. A moment more and they would all be doomed. Lifting her skirt to her ankle she released her dagger from its casing and the next moment the dagger had plunged itself into Sir Drakes neck. His piercing scream was all that was needed for the steeds to bolt.

"My Lady, do not stop no matter what ye hear or see. Go to Kinsborough. My Lord Raul waits to wed ye again." Emma did not have the time to ask him what he meant.

"I will remain with Lady Emma. God speed in yer task ahead." Rosalie spoke to Rowan

With one last look at each of them, Rowan slapped their steed's rump. The next minute the two women were racing back along the path they came.

The clang of swords could be heard loudly no matter how far they rode, but they dared not turn and look for fear of what they might see.

They raced for some miles and thought themselves clear of danger when suddenly the flash of red appeared again. The dagger still pierced to the side of his neck, Drake chased them, until his steed rode beside hers.

"Lady Clarissa, did ye really think ye were smarter than yer father and brother. One died in an accident, the other in a battle, clearing my path to Roseborough. Only ye stand now between Roseborough and me. If I cannot have Roseborough with ye, I will take it without ye. Do ye want me to end it for ye the way I ended it for yer father? The way I ended it for yer brother." he taunted.

"Nay! Ye lie." Emma screamed. Both murdered, by this man.

"Would ye like me to tell ye how it was done? Yer father was easy; ambushed by bandits as he came to arrest me.

Yer brother was harder. We fought alongside, but only I knew that the enemy that struck him was me."

"Why do ye tell me all this now?" she asked tortured at the revelations.

"Because it is the same courtesy I extended to yer father. He knew he was going to die and he knew who was going to kill him and how."

"Why did ye let me live then?" she asked

"I wanted Roseborough. I could not find the parchment he left. The only way to claim Roseborough was by wedding ye, so I claimed guardianship."

"The King did not give ye guardianship?" she asked.

"Nay but I got his seal." he boasted.

"What ye did to my kin was murder, what ye do to our Sire, is treason." she uttered with tears streaming down her face.

"Do ye not consider it treason when the King leaves England in the care of others and spends years on foreign soil fighting a hopeless battle? Is it not treason against his country to leave it without its Sire?" he countered.

"Did ye send the missive from the Sire to My Lord as well?" she queried.

"What missive?"

"Our sire is here." she informed him hoping to distract him long enough to make another move.

"Ye jest again. First ye claim to be Lord Kinsborough's bride, now ye claim the King is here. Enough, ye will come with me now." He rode closer.

"Touch her and ye forfeit yer life."

The sweetest words echoed in her ears. He had come; her lord had come.

"Aah another champion! Her first champion has been disposed of already, now ye line up for yer death." Drake snarled at Raul.

"Not just one, Sir Drake. Ye left behind one more." another voice reached Emma's ears. It could not be. Andrew was dead. As she turned to look towards the sound, Sir Drake reached for her, dislodging her from her steed.

"What is it with ye and yer men, Sir Drake. Ye tend not to heed to a warning. I said, touch her and ye forfeit yer life. Like yer men, ye do not heed the spoken word?" Raul growled.

"And who might ye be to issue such a warning?" he turned to Raul.

"I believe Sir Andrew's brother by marriage." Raul replied.

"Ye lie too. She claimed she was already wed, and now ye make that claim too. Who are ye?" Sir Drake asked.

"Lady Clarissa's lord, Lady Emma's husband, and Baron of Kinsborough." he replied.

From the corner of his eyes Raul saw Emma start as he used her real name. Drake was visibly shaken.

"Lady Clarissa will not be yers. Never yers.", and with that Sir Drake raised his sword.

In the next instant, Peter's lance had pierced Sir Drake's chest. Emma heard the thud as his body fell off his steed.

"My Lords, as defender to Lady Emma, it was my right. I am also the only one of the three of us who the Sire, had not forbidden to act." Peter gave Raul a smile that claimed his right. Peter knew, had a brother or husband acted, it could have been called murder.

"Sir Peter, I thank ye both for saving me and for saving the two that I love." Emma spoke.

For Andrew, her words were a confirmation, for Raul, it was a revelation. His bride had just used the word, love. And more wondrously, she had not even realised that she had said it. As if the word love and her feeling, had long been united.

While Raul lived with his thoughts Emma had run and thrown herself into her brother's arms.

"I cannot believe it, ye live." She spoke.

Raul stayed seated on Daktonian and watched the brother and sister. Now that the danger was over, another presented itself. The truth about their, unwed status! With her brother back, would she now choose to return to Roseborough?

"My Lord!" Rosalie addressed Raul.

"Aye?" he questioned.

"Sir Rowan and four knights fight twice as many mercenaries." She spoke.

"They have help Rosalie. It was they, who alerted us that Sir Drake was missing." he informed.

"My Lord, while brother and sister meet, I wish to unburden a truth as well." Rosalie spoke.

That got Raul's interest. "Unburden what truth? Pray do not tell me ye were party to this." he queried.

"Nay My Lord, but I have been a silent witness to a greater crime." she replied.

"What crime?" he interrogated.

"The night yer mother fell from the rampart another was seen coming down the stairwell. One, who claimed, that she was not in the castle. The new Lady of Wilbert."

"Rosalie, how can that be? My mother's fall was an accident." Raul felt the hair on his arms stand on end. He had always suspected but could not broach the subject without proof.

"My mother revealed once that she had overheard Lord Wilbert refuse to leave yer mother. He told the new lady that their relationship could continue, but his marriage would prevail."

"Why did yer mother not speak up?" he asked.

"My mother disappeared soon after yer mother's death. Everyone said it was the sea that took her, but My Lord, if it did, then the sea found a way to silence the truth forever." she replied.

Raul ran his fingers through his hair. When he looked up, Emma stood in front of Daktonian. They too had heard all.

"My Lord, ye need to save yer father." she said

"And ye My Lady, do ye come with me?" he asked, with words that spoke with double intent.

Before Emma could reply, men on steeds came from all directions. Rowan and his knights! Peter's men! And from the direction of Kinsborough, came their Sire.

Not one knight had been lost, but Emma saw, that many had been wounded.

Before the king reached them, Emma moved closer to Raul and said, "My Lord, tonight I will remain at Kinsborough, for the sick room will be well occupied. Tomorrow My Lord, tomorrow I will follow ye."

"And yer desire to go the Abbey of St Mary?" he asked.

"My brother proceeds to retrieve the parchments. It is being held in the Abbey for us. My father knew what was to befall and prepared his move to outwit Drake."

Raul smiled but was unable to respond for the King and his party had reached them.

Turning to her sire, Emma made a low courtesy, "My Sire!" she said.

"Lady Emma. Ye have made for a merry chase." he smiled, noting that Raul had marked his use of the name Emma and not Clarissa.

"Believe me sire, the chase was not of my making." she replied not refuting the address.

Her sire burst out laughing "Baron Raul let me tell ye how yer bride came to get the name Emma. I christened her Lady Emma, Healer of the Universe, for she was ever by the side of a physician wanting to heal."

"Sire, when a king calls his subject by a name, does that name not become a lawful one as well?" he queried the King but gave Emma a smile that said, this time ye are bested.

"It is as true as my title. Ye talk of yer bride's little charade, do ye not?" the king asked.

"Aye sire, she claims we are unwed for she signed her name as Emma" he addressed the king.

"Baron Raul, ye waste time, arguing with a woman. If ye do not have a friar I have one with me. Wed her again tonight. If she is not yer bride, she is still my ward and I command it." The King challenged Emma.

"Lady Emma its yers to decide, do ye remain wed as Lady Emma or do I marry Lady Clarissa?" Raul posed the question to his bride.

"What of the Order of the Templar Knight? Was it not yer desire?" she asked.

"It was." he acknowledged, noting the sadness that entered her eyes "It is, no longer" he ended.

If he considered her eyes the most beautiful before, he had cause to reinstate that view.

"Baron Raul, take the women and return to yer castle and prepare for a feast. There is much to celebrate. A brother found his sister, a husband won his bride, a lady exposed a murder and a man was killed for treason. Tomorrow ye both can sort out yer family issues. If what was just told is true, Lord Wilbert's second bride will receive her just punishment."

"I will send out an order for the banishment of Lady Maja and her children." The king added.

"Sire, she had no children." Raul corrected.

"Did yer father not know? Maja has a son and a daughter being brought up by their uncle. She was once mistress to an earl, a cousin of mine." The King who equally loved to tell of gossip as to hear of it, revealed further.

The king's declaration stunned everyone. Raul now saw clearly why Maja was determined to see him wed her niece. She would have been mother to his bride had he agreed. And her son would have claimed Wilbert, had he not.

Raul remembered Rosalie's words. 'Do not underestimate Lady Wilbert' He would go to Wilbert tomorrow. It was time Maja left his mother's home. This time he would enter Wilbert with the royal seal of approval.

Chapter 22

During the feast that night, Raul and Emma explained the past to Sir Andrew. They told of the whole truth, of their meeting and the reason they wed.

"So ye bid for her?" Andrew asked.

"I had no choice. Too many were armed and yer sister remained bound." Raul explained

"Ye were fortunate; it is my sister ye bid on. And my sister was blessed ye rescued her." Andrew said.

"I am honoured ye think so Andrew." Raul replied with humility.

Emma's attension was taken by King Richard who wanted to discuss her plans for the sick room. As they got deeply involved in their conversation, Andrew leaned across and asked.

"Raul, I leave tomorrow for the Abbey and Roseborough too needs caring. Before I go, I need to know ye love her for it seems ye still share a strange marriage." Andrew spoke in a low tone.

"That is no longer of my choosing. It was easier to bid for my bride than it was to earn her love." Raul replied.

"Mayhaps instead of earning her love, ye need to bid on it. It is obvious ye gamble with luck" Andrew jested back in hushed tones.

"Aye that is a good thought, mayhaps, I will bid on her love." Raul laughed.

Music and dance followed supper. The king accustomed to the luxury of his palace, none the less, enjoyed the meal and the music. Emma's first dance was with her sire. At the end of which he handed her back to Raul.

As Raul danced with Emma, she asked "Ye shared many laughs with my brother, what did ye both discuss?"

"Yer brother suggested I bid on yer love." he said.

"Why would Andrew suggest that My Lord?" she questioned.

"He agrees, it is easier that winning a lady's heart." he replied.

"Nay My Lord 'bid not for my love', for it is already freely given." she replied.

Raul gazed into her eyes and it clearly said, "I am ready to be yer bride."

As he moved a step closer she stopped him with her words.

"And ye, do ye still wish to become a Templar Knight?"

"Nay my love! I will pledge my aid with coin and support but I plan to withdraw my request to serve in the Order." Raul told.

"And will our sire agree?" she asked.

"We will know later." he replied.

'Then My Lord, it is best we decide our future then."

"I do not understand. Ye wish to remain wed, do ye not?" he queried.

"My Lord, my pledge was to the Baron not the Templar Knight. It will remain only to the Baron." she clarified.

It was an answer that both pleased him and caused him concern. Much rested on their Sire's decision.

After supper, as the merry making continued, Raul approached the king.

"Sire, I come with a difficult request." he started

"What is it Baron Raul? What do ye seek now, having already wed my ward?" the king asked.

"Sire, I seek to be released from my request. I no longer wish to join the Templar Knights. I will pledge my help to raise coins and maintain yer stronghold in England, but I am unable to offer a pledge to the Templar Knights."

"This is precisely the reason why the 'Order of the Templar' wants to forbid its knights to wed. A wedded man is a weakened man." The Kings sounded disappointed.

"Sire, my bride is not the only reason. I have both Wilbert and Kinsborough to care for." he informed.

"Aye Aye, I am aware of it. I cannot take all my warriors with me for that will weaken England. Keep England safe for me then and protect my throne." The king commanded.

"Aye Sire, that pledge I give with all my heart. Ye borders will remain safe." he pledged.

"Ye are excused then Baron Raul. Go be a real husband. That will be yer crusade."

Laughing at his own joke, the king continued. "And ye can give me much for the crusades for ye wed one that brings rich coffers with her."

At seeing Raul frown, the King continued, "She brings two castles and a chest of gold coins."

Raul was stunned to hear this. He had bought an heiress for mere coins, and now she had enough to buy him and his castle. And by giving a part of her gold for the crusade, she was effectively buying him his freedom. Had not he told her once 'Maybe one day ye can return the favour'.

That night after the merry making ended, and Emma had checked on the knights in the sick room with the physician, she returned to her room. Raul was already there, resting against the wall.

"My Lady, it seems, we have to share the room again, for our Sire has taken mine." he remarked.

"It would not surprise me, if ye gave our sire yer room with intent." she replied.

"And why would I do that, My Lady?" he queried.

"So ye can vex me." she replied with annoyance.

Raul laughed. "It seems My Lady is easily vexed".

"It is the quality I inherited when I wed thee" she retorted but continued to smile.

"Tomorrow our sire leaves and we ride with him" he said next.

"For, what purpose, My Lord?" Emma inquired.

"Like ye, my mother was a royal ward. Her murder will be avenged by the royal's son. We will return once Wilbert has been liberated from her clutches." he answered in a somber tone.

"And, the Lord of Wilbert, what of his attachment to the lady?" Emma asked.

"As ye rightly said, in his heart he must know the truth of it. Maximillian informed me that my father had not been aware of Maja's trip to Wilbert at the time of my mother's death. Now with my father ailing, Maja must have seen desperation before her! His death would mean the end of her rule at Wilbert. I was to be her next prey in her last attempt to hold on to what she had."

"What of Wilbert?" she asked.

"It will remain as it exists while my father dwells there. After him, our sire has suggested it be turned into a place to care for the sick and the injured. It seems he was impressed with yer views and takes credit for making ye 'the true healer of the universe."

"Nay My Lord, Leave Wilbert for yer son, I have a castle that would suit better." she suggested.

"My son? Ye promise to give me one, do ye?" he asked as he looked at the woman who had stolen his heart.

"Nay My Lord!" she replied and then with a twinkle in her eyes and laughter in her voice added "I promise to give ye, one for each castle."

And she looked at the knight, who in so short a time had become the man she would love forever.

"Then I need build more castles very soon, if ye plan to compete with their numbers." he said, his warm eyes promising her the impossible.

"Nay My Lord, three will be quite enough. Yer eldest will take Kinsborough, yer second Wilbert and yer daughter will take mine. If ye wish to construct more, then ye can build more sick rooms for us."

"Us?" he questioned

"Ye and me, My Lord." she replied.

"My name be Raul, Emma" he said, giving her the liberty few brides were given in his time.

"When tomorrow we return, My Lord, then ye shall be my Raul. For one last night, ye can gloat, at being 'My Lord.'" She bantered.

His laughter echoed in her ears even as she woke the next morning, to a new life that promised to be what dreams are truly made of.

The End

Made in the USA
Middletown, DE
26 October 2020

22560171R00146